THE TRAIL TO RETRIBUTION

PLAINSMAN WESTERN SERIES BOOK NINE

B.N. RUNDELL

The Trail to Retribution
Paperback Edition

Wolfpack Publishing
9850 S. Maryland Parkway, Suite A-5 #323
Las Vegas, Nevada 89183

wolfpackpublishing.com

Paperback ISBN 978-1-63977-259-9
Large Print Hardcover ISBN 978-1-63977-260-5
eBook ISBN 978-1-63977-258-2

To those who have given their lives for our freedoms, from the earliest days of the birth of our nation, through the many wars and conflicts and even on this day. Whether your uniform was green, khaki, blue, grey, or any other color, and to those who continue to give their time, energies, and blood so that we may live without fear and enjoy the freedom we have in this, the greatest nation on earth. God bless you one and all.

THE TRAIL TO RETRIBUTION

1 / VALLEY

The big cow elk tiptoed from the timber, head high, smelling the wind and all it carried. A few tentative steps more, looking around as she walked into the highlands on the east edge of the vast San Luis Valley, and quickened her step, going to water in the little creek that still carried runoff from the snowmelt high in the Sangre de Cristo mountains. A quick look over her shoulder and several other elk followed, cows with new calves romping in the belly-deep grass and greasewood, and a few yearling bulls sporting velvet covered spikes. They moved through the brush with a proprietary confidence for they were the largest animals in the woods, save the grizzly.

Reuben Grundy sat his blue roan gelding, leaning on the pommel with forearms crossed as he watched. He looked to the side and smiled at his woman, Elly, aboard her leopard Appaloosa mare who was rapt and smiling as she watched this phenomenon of the Rockies. She let a soft giggle escape, "I will *never* get tired of seeing that! They are such magnificent creatures!"

The sudden blast of a rifle shot made them and their

horses flinch as the small herd of elk jerked away from the sound, turned on their heels, and with great long strides and lunges disappeared back into the thick black timber that skirted the granite-tipped peaks of the Sangres. Both Reuben and Elly stood in their stirrups, peering through the opening in the pines, to see the shooter rise from the brush, look around, and start slowly to the downed yearling, the larger of the two young bulls. Reuben frowned, "He's just a kid!" He turned as he pointed, looking to Elly, "You see that? He's just a kid and looks like he's all alone!"

Elly nodded, looked at the youngster pushing his way through the greasewood brush, his rifle cradled in the crook of his left arm, and focused on his kill. "Let's go down there, if he's alone he could use some help."

As they pushed their mounts from the trees, Reuben called out, "Hello down there!" It was never a wise thing to ride up on an unsuspecting armed man and the code of the wilderness demanded you announce your presence. The young man froze in place and lifted his rifle to his shoulder, but kept the muzzle pointed to the ground, "What'chu want? This is my kill! I shot him!"

"We know. Not disputing that. Thought you might need some help, that's all."

The two riders drew near, both keeping their free hand about waist-high, showing they were not brandishing any weapons. Elly asked, "Are you alone?"

The young man frowned, looking from Reuben to Elly, obviously surprised to see a woman. He stammered a mite, "Uh, no! My pa's back yonder, he'll be comin' along soon!"

Both Reuben and Elly looked beyond the boy and his kill, saw nothing in the brush, nothing on the far side of the creek and back at the boy. Reuben nodded to Elly, and both stepped down, Elly approaching with a broad smile, "I'm Elly, and this is my husband, Deputy Marshal Reuben Grundy. And you are...?"

Reuben stayed by the horses and their pack mule that most always roamed free rein and began tethering the animals to a thicket of greasewood. He turned to look at the boy as the youngster asked, "You really a deputy marshal?"

Reuben grinned, reached into the pocket of his jacket and brought out the marshal's badge to show it to the young man, "Yup, but so's she!" nodding to Elly who also produced a marshal's badge.

"Unnhnn, ain't no woman no marshal!" he declared, shaking his head. He had yet to lower his rifle and looked suspiciously from Elly to Reuben.

Elly chuckled and smiled, nodding, "Well, this time there is. You see, when my husband was asked by Ben Holladay and Marshal Moses to become a deputy, he said he would as long as I could be with him, so, they made me a deputy as well. Now, I don't do as much as he does, I'm just kinda along for the ride, so..." she shrugged, giving the boy a bit of a conspiratorial smile and a wink. "Now, what's your name?"

"Uh, uh, I'm Joel, Joel Schmidt. Did you mean it when you said you came to help?"

"Yes, of course," replied Elly, turning to smile at Reuben so he would come closer and help. Elly walked to the downed elk, saw the blood where the bullet struck, and turned to Joel, "My, that was a good shot, Joel! Right through the heart!"

The boy grinned, sat his rifle down, butt first, and leaned it against the head of the elk, dropped to one knee and pulled his knife from the sheath at his belt, and looked at Elly, "I always hit where I aim. Pa says I'm a natural good shot!" he proclaimed proudly.

"I can see that." She slipped her knife from the scabbard that hung between her shoulder blades and as Reuben lifted the hind leg, she began cutting the hide to open the animal from tail to chin and begin field dressing the bull. The boy watched as she began then inserted his knife just under the chin and began his cut, intending to meet hers in the middle. As they worked, Reuben asked, "You wanna save the hide in one piece?"

"Uh, yeah, I s'pose," replied Joel, looking at Reuben as he held the leg high, giving Elly room to work.

"Your pa tan the hide?" asked Elly, focusing on her work.

The young man paused, frowned, "I don't remember him doin' it, but he musta, cuz we got some tanned hides in the wagon. But we ain't had none lately, so..." he cocked his head to the side, shrugged, and resumed his cutting.

He followed Elly's lead and as the cut met in the middle, Elly stood and looked up at Reuben with a smile, "I'll trade ya!"

Reuben chuckled, let her take the leg and traded places as Joel continued to peel the hide back, using his knife carefully to cut the membrane between the meat and the hide. Reuben opened the stomach cavity and reached in to pull out the innards and slide them into a pile, cut the membrane and more to free the gut pile and drug the innards aside. He cut the kidney free, tossed it to their big black dog, "Here ya go, Bear!" and watched the dog jump in the air to catch the thrown morsel and carry it away to enjoy his feast.

"That's a big dog!" declared Joel who had sat back on his haunches to watch.

In short order, they had stripped the hide, laid it hair down and piled the four quarters of meat on top. They stood back, looking at the stack and Reuben looked at Joel, "So, where's your pa?"

Joel hung his head and mumbled, "Back at the wagon. He's all stove up."

Elly frowned, stepped beside the youngster who appeared to be all of twelve years old, and lay her hand on his shoulder, "I kinda guessed there was something like that. What happened?"

Joel looked up at both Reuben and Elly, "We was comin' up from the valley of the Arkansas," nodding to the north end of the San Luis Valley, "an' after we topped out, somethin' spooked the horses and they started runnin'. Took a while for Pa to get 'em stopped, but just as they was slowin', the wagon hit a big rock an' busted a wheel. When Pa tried fixin' it, the wagon fell on him, broke a leg, and hurt the other'n. Me'n Ma had to work real hard to get him out from under, an' mighta broke his arm in the doin' of it." He shook his head, sobbed, and daubed at tears that filled his eyes as he hung his head. "We been without meat an' I been out ever' day." He nodded to the pile before them, "This is the first!"

Elly pulled him close, hugging him as she said, "We'll help you get this back to 'em and see if we can help out a mite." She pushed him away to look at him, both hands on his shoulders, "Would that be alright?"

A slow smile parted his tear-stained face and he nodded enthusiastically. "Yes'm."

The mule had been packed light but now carried most of the meat, while the hide and the rest of the meat was divided between the two horses. Joel was seated atop the folded hide behind Elly's saddle, while Reuben's roan carried the rest of the meat. Joel had walked most of three miles from their camp and as they neared the tree line, they could see the pale wagon cover showing through the trees. Joel called out, "Ma! Ma! It's me! I got meat! And some friends!" He spoke softly to Elly, "If I didn't call, she'd shoot first and ask questions after! She can't hit nuthin' but she's got Pa's shotgun and she'll use it!"

"Well, let's hope she heard you!" answered Elly, glancing to a grinning Reuben.

As they broke through the trees, the campsite showed sign of an extended stay. Two trunks sat behind the wagon, a couple boxes, probably used for seating, sat on the far side of the fire circle, and a woman in a long gingham dress stood with the shotgun held low, as she watched them come close. She lifted her left hand to shade her eyes, frowned, and said, "Where you at boy?"

"Here, Ma!" declared Joel, leaning to the side to show himself behind Elly. She offered her hand and he accepted her help as he slid to the ground, leaving his rifle behind the cantle of the saddle as he ran to his mother. "Ma! I got some meat! Lots of it!"

She nodded, keeping her eyes on the two strangers, and motioned, "You can step down if you're of a mind."

"Thank you," answered Elly, glancing to Reuben who was stepping down and came to her side to give her a hand, not that she needed it, but just showing courtesy, as was his way. Elly slid to the ground, and into his arms, and with a smile to her man, stepped aside and started to the woman. She extended her hand and smiled, "I'm Elly Grundy, and this," nodding to Reuben, "is my husband, Reuben." She smiled at Joel, "We gave your son a hand butchering his elk and thought we might see if we could be of help to you."

"Why?" she asked, frowning, and holding the shotgun tight to her side.

"Well, Joel told us what happened, and we were there, so…" she shrugged.

"Whatchu want?" growled the woman, starting to lift the shotgun.

"Ma! They're deputy marshals, Ma! They helped me!" he declared, frowning at his mother. Movement at the wagon caught their attention and Joel ran to the wagon to help his father, "Pa! Tell Ma to put the shotgun down! She's scary with that thing!"

The man had been under the wagon on some blankets and sat up to lean against the wheel. His splinted leg stretched out before him, and a bandaged arm held across his chest. He looked at the two strangers, nodded to his woman who relaxed her grip on the shotgun but did not sit it down. "Thank you for helpin' my boy! As you can see, I ain't much help to nobody!"

Elly frowned, looked at the woman, and said, "Maybe I could be of help? I've done some fixin' of bones and such."

"Why?"

"Why? Well, because it looks like he could use some help."

The woman took a deep breath that lifted her shoulders and glanced to her husband, "You want she should look at'chu?"

"Can't hurt none," he nodded.

Elly glanced to Reuben, and both walked to the wagon, Elly going to one knee beside the man. As she did, he looked at her, "I'm Jared, Jared Schmidt." He smiled, lifted his eyes to his wife and spoke louder, "And that cranky ol' woman over there is my loving wife, Gertrude!" and chuckled.

The woman shook her head, fighting to keep from smiling and chuckled, "That's me, alright. Since that happened, things have gone from bad to worse and it just didn't seem possible there would be good folks willing to help, just cuz!" She sat the shotgun down, went to the fire and picked up a couple cups, poured them full of coffee, and took them to the visitors. "Pardon me for bein' suspicious, it's just that..." she shook her head as tears filled her eyes. She lifted the edge of her apron and daubed at the tears, turning away to hide her embarrassment.

Elly smiled, "I understand. Sometimes it seems kindness is harder to find than a deposit of gold! Ought not to be that way, but I guess it's the times we're livin' in, what with the war and all."

2 / FRIENDS

While Elly and Gertrude tended to Jared's injuries, Reuben and Joel looked over the busted wheel and the wagon, now propped up on one corner. Reuben looked down at Joel, "What'chu think? Think we can fix it?"

"Don't need ta fix it, just replace it with the extry wheel we got," answered the young man, nodding to the wheel leaning against the big aspen.

"Well, let me have a better look. I think I need to crawl under and have a look at that axle," explained Reuben, dropping to his knees beside the wagon. They were on the far side from the women and Jared, and Reuben bent down, looked at the axle, crawled underneath for a better look, and gave a quick check of the rest of the wagon box and running gear. Everything seemed to be in order, no obvious damage, and he worked his way from under the box and stood beside the boy. He nodded to the wheel and they both went to the trees and examined the spare wheel. "This looks to be in fine shape," and with a glance to the boy he added, "Your pa got a bucket o' grease?"

"Ummhmm," answered Joel, nodding to the bucket hanging at the side of the wagon.

"Then looks like all we need is a fulcrum and lever to lift the wagon."

Joel frowned, "A what?"

"I'll show you. First, we need some flat rocks, the bigger the better. And then we'll need a good-sized pole," he spoke as he walked into the trees, looking about for a suitable tree to make a lever or beam that would be used to lift the wagon. As they walked, Reuben asked, "What'd your dad use before to lift the wagon?"

"He had part of a broken tongue from another wagon, but it slipped and that's when the wagon came down on Pa's leg." The boy chuckled, grinning, "Pa's a good man an' Ma don't let him use no bad language, but he sure wanted to that day! He was growlin' and moanin' sumpin' awful! His face turned red an' ever'thing!" declared Joel, shaking his head, and fighting the grin that wanted to surface. He knew his pa's injury was not a laughing matter and he shouldn't make fun but remembering his dad's expression won out and he grinned as he followed Reuben.

"That looks good!" declared Reuben, pointing to a lodgepole pine that showed grey with several dead branches and nothing showing green. It was a standing dead snag, probably winter kill, and would be strong enough if it wasn't rotted.

Reuben stepped near, looking up and down the trunk of the tall, straight tree, the same kind used by the native people for their lodgepoles, thus the name. He slipped his metal bladed hatchet from his belt and began chopping at the trunk about a foot above ground level and soon had the tree toppled. He handed the hatchet to Joel, "You wanna trim off the branches?"

The boy grinned, nodding as he reached for the hatchet and began chopping at the dead branches and stubs of branches. As Reuben watched, he was pleased to see the boy properly wielding the hand axe, always careful with the cut, ensuring it was from the bottom of the branch upwards so as not to split the wood. Within a few moments, the trunk was trimmed and sized, cut to length and Reuben nodded to the small end, "How 'bout you take that end and we'll get back to the wagon?"

Joel quickly returned the hatchet and went to the upper end of the trunk and the two workers carried it back to the camp. After gathering several flat limestone slide-rocks, they soon had their fulcrum and lever. Reuben positioned everything, readying to lift the wagon. With the spare wheel in place beside the wagon box, the axle greased, and everyone in place, the work began. With Jared using his weight on the fulcrum, the women assisting him to stabilize the pole, Reuben readied the wheel. The wagon slowly lifted, "A little more, a little more," instructed Reuben, keeping his eyes on the hub and the wagon as the others lifted. He motioned to Joel, "Boy, quickly pull that box out," motioning to the box that had sat atop the rock to hold the wagon level. Joel grabbed the rope handle and tugged, slowly slipping the box away as Reuben lifted and leaned the wheel to the axle.

"Now, hold it steady, just a moment!" as he positioned the hub to the axle and lifted it just enough to slip it onto the end of the skein. "Almost got it!" Reuben pushed the wheel tight and put the nut on, tightened it down, "Alright! You can let 'er down!" he hollered, stepping back from the wagon. As they slowly lowered the wagon, the new wheel took its weight and stood firm. They pulled out the fulcrum and let it lay. The women helped Jared back to his seat on the log by the fire ring and everyone looked around, smiling and relieved the work was done.

Jared looked at Reuben, "I'm mighty grateful for your help. Couldn'ta done it without'cha. At least not for a spell, anyhow."

Reuben let a bit of a smile tug at the corners of his mouth and looked over at Joel, "And we couldn't have done it without Joel there, and the women folk. Takes everyone pitchin' in, sometimes, and the Lord has a way of bringin' help, just when we need it most."

Gertrude and Elly had gone to the fire to stir up the coals for some hot coffee and Gertrude spoke up, "Amen to that!" eliciting a chuckle from a smiling Elly.

"I'll say," she agreed, smiling at Gertrude and nodding.

Gertrude lowered her voice as she slowly shook her head, "That stubborn ol' goat doesn't wanna give the Lord credit for anything! But now…" she smiled, "just say you are a godsend."

While the men talked about plans, work, futures, and the weather, the women were rummaging around to plan the next meal. Gertrude glanced at Elly, "I'm sorry we're so low on supplies. We been eatin' nuthin' but flap-jacks, corn dodgers, and beans for the last week or so."

Elly looked to Gertrude, "Have you folks been in the mountains long?"

"No. We came with a small wagon train after we left Ohio. We were loaded up good then, but we're gettin' low on just about everything. Don't know what we're gonna do," she explained, daubing at a tear as she struggled to maintain her composure. "I just haven't had a woman to talk to for nigh on a month now, maybe longer."

Elly smiled, "You got a basket, bucket, something like that?" and stood up, looking about.

"Uh, yeah," answered Gertrude, frowning as she went to the wagon to fetch both a wooden bucket and a small basket.

Elly grinned when she returned, looked to the men, and said, "We'll be back in a bit!" She slipped her Henry from the scabbard, used the leather sling to put it over her shoulder, and nodded to Gertrude, "Let's go shopping!"

As they walked from the tree line toward the creek below, Elly began pointing out different plants, some harvestable in the spring, others that would be available later. "There's some columbine," she began, starting to a small cluster of blue blossoms with white centers. She plucked some of the blooms, "These are good," as she bit into the petals, "just as they are, or as part of a salad. Many spring blossoms are like that."

"I've used some flower petals from our garden, but not like this," proclaimed Gertrude, picking a handful.

"And look here," said Elly as she walked to a rocky mound with thin leafed and white blossomed plants catching the sunlight. "These are Indian potatoes! The root bulbs are the best."

As they continued their walk, Elly pointed out some plants with a long thin stem and flat white flowers beginning to blossom, "These are Yampa and their root bulbs are best – late summer, early fall. They can be dried and made into a flour, but the bulbs are best baked in the coals."

She spotted some onions, began digging some as she explained, "Natives use these for cuts and burns, and one woman said they also use them for male impotency!" she giggled as she plucked some more.

Their harvesting walk continued as they came to a backwater of the creek where a thicket of cattail stood and she smiled as she began to explain the uses of the shoots, roots, and flower heads, "And the pollen can be used for a flour also!" she proclaimed. The women strolled along the creek bank, each learning from the other and forming a bond of friendship that would be enjoyed and appreciated by both women.

It was a casual walk and a comfortable time of learning and sharing, until Elly stopped and bent low, motioning for Gertrude to do the same. They were near the willows on the creek bank and stepped closer to the thicket as Elly slowly rose to look across the creek and into the grassy plain. She counted eight riders, all warriors, probably Ute. She looked as long as she dared, trying to identify the men as Ute or Jicarilla Apache, or even Comanche. But there was nothing that she could see from the distance that convinced her of any tribe. She knew this was the territory of the Ute, Tabeguache and Caputa mostly, but other tribes hunted this land as well. She watched as they rode on, siding the lower slope where the greenery faded into the dusty shades of purple, grey, and tans of the sage, greasewood, and buffalo grass.

She whispered to Gertrude, "Let's stay low and get back to camp," and started up the long slope in a crouch, moving as quickly as possible carrying the wooden bucket and basket full of their harvest. Gertrude stayed close and within moments the women were in the trees and stopped, stood, and looked back to see if the party of Indians had gone. With a long sigh of relief, the women looked at one another, smiled, and turned toward the camp and quickly sought its cover.

Reuben saw his wife's expression and knew she was

concerned. He stood, stepped closer, "What is it?" he asked, reaching out for the bucket and her hands. He put the bucket down, looked at her, and glanced to Gertrude, "What'd you see?"

She started to speak, but Gertrude spouted, "Indians! A bunch of 'em!"

Reuben looked at her, back to Elly to see his wife nod and with eyes wide, "But I'm sure they did not see us. There were eight of them and I think they were Ute but were too far to be sure. No pack animals, no game, so they might just be starting a hunt."

"Prob'ly. But we need to be cautious anyway." He looked around the camp, "And it wouldn't hurt to build a few breastworks, you know, some cover, just in case." He glanced to Jared, "With you hobbled a mite, you'll probably be here a while and some cover would be good." He glanced to the wagon, "And that," nodding to the pale canvas cover, "shows through the trees. It'd be good to either cover it, lower it, or somethin'." And so began their fortification of the camp.

3 / VISITORS

Reuben was an experienced woodsman and well-armed. Having served with Berdan's Sharpshooters in the beginning of the Civil War, he had proven himself in the woods and as an excellent marksman. Standing just over six feet tall, long blonde hair that hung almost to his broad shoulders, deep chested and muscular, he had repeatedly proven himself as a fighter experienced in free-for-all fighting with his brothers and fellow soldiers. His weapons of choice were his Sharps rifle with telescopic sights, a Henry rifle, a Remington Army revolver that hung in a holster on his left hip, and a Bowie knife in a sheath between his shoulder blades. A metal bladed tomahawk or hatchet sat in his belt on his right hip. Beaded and fringed buckskins were his preferred attire, although he sometimes wore the woolen britches of the Berdan uniform.

Elly, a blue-eyed blonde at just over five feet, covered her petite form with a braided buckskin tunic and leggings over beaded high-topped moccasins. She had a Colt Pocket pistol holstered on her left hip, a Flemish knife in a sheath between her shoulder blades, and a

Henry rifle in the scabbard of her saddle. Her horse was a leopard Appaloosa mare she called Daisy, and she was seldom apart from the big black dog she called Bear because of his resemblance to the beast of the same name and about the same size.

As they worked together to bring stones, branches, and logs to build breastworks for the camp, their confident manner lent a comforting assurance to the camp and their new friends, the Schmidts. As they worked, Reuben told the Schmidts about their experience with different native bands, "And the Ute are usually friendly with the settlers. One band that lives across the valley there, are known as the Tabeguache. Their chief is Ouray, a good leader who has worked long and hard to bring peace to his people. Right now, most of them are camped at Fort Garland trying to work out a peace treaty with the soldiers. But there are others, the Mouache and the Capute that don't necessarily agree with Ouray and aren't as friendly. We just spent some time with the Mouache and their chief, Kaniache. There was a little fracas down to the south end of the valley, some white men lookin' for gold in all the wrong places."

"What about this land?" asked Jared. "We can settle here, can't we?"

"Well…it's still the land of the Tabeguache and not officially open for settlement, although some have already begun to build their homes and such. There were early settlers, Mexican mostly, that came north with their sheep, after the war with Mexico was settled, into the south end of the valley, and the new boundaries were in place, but they pretty much made peace with the Ute and Jicarilla. But with the gold rush north of here, there's been more prospectors and gold hunters as well as settlers comin' into the valley." Reuben looked up at

Jared and asked, "Were you thinkin' more of settling, maybe farming, or were you lookin' for gold?"

Jared chuckled as he dropped his eyes, "If I find gold, it'll be while I'm plowin' or clearin' land. I don't know the first thing 'bout lookin' for gold. But this land 'tween here an' the crick, looks good, but I'm thinkin' it's more for raisin' stock than crops."

"My folks were farmers back in Michigan territory, 'fore the war. But that country is a lot different than this country." Reuben nodded to the mountains behind them that still held spots of snow in the high peaks, "and I'm no farmer, but with everything else gettin' so green, surely there's some crops that'd grow this high. The commandant down at Fort Garland said he thought this upper end of the valley was 'tween 7,000 and 8,000 feet. The rainfall here is nothin' like what they get on the east side of the Mississippi."

As the men talked of the land, Reuben kept watching through the trees for any visitors. Movement caught his attention and he paused, stepping closer to the tree line, and shielded behind a thick aspen, he watched several riders move slowly along the embankment of the lower creek. He called over his shoulder, "Elly, get my Sharps and the scope!" He turned to watch the riders, now a good 800 yards away, but as he watched, they stopped, gathered into a group, and talked animatedly, gesturing to the tree line where he waited.

Elly came alongside, nudged him with the Sharps and he accepted the rifle, keeping his eyes on the riders, now identifiable as warriors, probably Ute. "Do those look like the same ones you saw earlier?"

She stepped beside him, shaded her eyes, and looked, "Hard to say, they're too far away. But how many bands like that are wandering around this valley?"

Reuben chuckled, looked at his smiling woman, and shook his head, "Yeah, I see what you mean!" He frowned, "Looks like just one of 'em's comin' our way."

With a glance over his shoulder, he spoke a little louder, "Jared! You and your family take cover but keep your weapons visible. There's one of 'em comin' closer, and we want 'em to think we've got plenty of rifles and shooters!" Jared nodded, spoke quietly to his wife and son, and they scampered for their weapons and to take cover as instructed.

Elly lifted the binoculars to take a better look, surprising Reuben that she had them, but he shook his head as he smiled at his woman, "What'chu see?"

"There's a white man with 'em."

"Captive?"

"No, but he's a scruffy one! He's talkin' to the others. I think he's tryin' to stir 'em up!"

The lone rider drew near, held one hand just above shoulder height, hand open and palm facing Reuben. An impressive figure, broad shouldered, with a hair-pipe bone breastplate, choker, and three feathers in his topknot. Loose hair hung over his shoulders, and Reuben noticed a gold nugget about the size of his thumb in the center of the breastplate. The leader stopped, "Maykw(a)."

Reuben stepped out, lifted his hand in a similar fashion, "Maykw(a)."

The warrior nodded, lowered his hand, and placed one on top of the other on the withers of his horse, leaned forward, scowled, and growled in English. "I am White Skunk of the Capote Ute people. You are on our land, you must leave," making a sweeping motion with his hand and arm as if wiping them away.

"I am Reuben, also known as Man with Blue Horse.

This," motioning to Elly who stood with her Henry cradled in her arms across her chest, "is my woman, Meadowlark, or Yellow Bird. We are friends with the Ute people. We know Ouray of the Tabeguache and Kaniache of the Mouache."

White Skunk snarled, "They are women!" He shook his head, glowered at Reuben, "You must leave, but we will take the wagon and all your things!"

Reuben let a slow grin split his face, chuckled, and shook his head, "You will take nothing but the bullets from our weapons!" He spoke softly but glared at the warrior. "You do not move!" demanded Reuben nodding toward Elly as she stepped forward, lifting her Henry to her shoulder, and raising the muzzle toward the warrior. Reuben glared at the man with a sneer and stated, "While you watch, I will shoot your warriors!"

"Ha! They are too far! You cannot shoot them and when you try, you will die!" snarled White Skunk, but he did not move, glancing to Elly and her rifle, literally looking down the barrel and seeing her resolve.

Reuben lifted his Sharps, leaned against the white bark of the aspen, brought the rifle to his shoulder, and took aim. As he held the rifle steady, he asked, "You want me to shoot the hat off that white man that's with you, or the buffalo skull cap on the other warrior?"

White Skunk scowled, twisted around to look back at the war party on the far side of the creek now about six hundred yards away. He looked back at Reuben, "The white man!"

Reuben grinned, took careful aim at the man's hat, confident in his ability for he had taken many such shots as an expert rifleman with Berdan's Sharpshooters, and slowly squeezed the thin trigger. The big rifle bucked and spat smoke and lead, and the man in the distance screamed, ducked, and grabbed his head. The hat had been sent sailing, and the furrow through his thick matted hair showed blood that began to drip down the man's forehead and pooled in his thick single eyebrow before dripping to the side of the whining man's nose.

White Skunk looked back at Reuben as Reuben said, "You want me to shoot another'n? But this time it'll be a kill shot?!"

"NO!" declared the startled warrior, squinting to look at the rifle in the man's hands, but Reuben set it down butt first, leaning it against his leg so the warrior could not easily see the weapon.

Reuben grinned at White Skunk, "That's just me, and the rest of these can do just as well, even the boy over there. Now, how 'bout you and your men skedaddle outta here and go find some four-legged animal that ain't affeered of you!"

White Skunk scowled, grumbled, and jerked the head of his horse around, dug heels and as the animal lunged, he lay low on the horse's neck and took off to his men at a run. Reuben turned to the others, "Get ready! They'll either leave or come chargin' in here. They been embarrassed and if they're smart, they'll leave, but there's no tellin' 'bout this bunch!" He nodded to Elly and they both walked back toward the wagon and the others.

4 / NOONING

The further north they traveled, the more the valley narrowed. The Sangre de Cristo mountains rimmed the east edge of the valley like a strong, insurmountable bastion that bent around the sand dunes and as it marched north, the neck of the valley narrowed to bring the Sangres to meet the foothills of the San Juans. Reuben and Elly took to the trail before the sun smiled over the mountain range and watched as it bent its golden shafts over the granite peaks to bring its life-giving warmth to the vast San Luis Valley. Elly drew alongside Reuben, "Do you really think they'll be alright?" she asked, pleading with her husband for reassurance.

"Elly, if you mean Jared and his family, we can't babysit every settler we come across, and yeah, they've had their problems, but Jared's getting better, especially after you tended to his broken leg and his scraped arm. The splint you put on helps him get around with those crutches I fashioned from the aspen saplings, and he can shoot. But Joel's a good shot and he can hunt and that

Gertrude, well, heaven help anybody, red or white, that'd try anything with her and that shotgun!"

"Well, I guess we did fix their wagon, and they're pretty well set up with their camp and such. Yeah, you're right. They'll probably be alright," she nodded, smiling. "And after those Capote Ute took off, I don't think they'll be comin' back."

"And unless I miss my guess, that," nodding to the trees some distance before them where steam could be seen rising into the morning sunlight, "is your hot springs!"

Elly stood in her stirrups, shaded her eyes from the long shafts of sunlight peeking over the mountains, smiled, and looked to Reuben, "I think you're right! I'm anxious to get in 'em too!" She had suffered a bullet wound from some rebellious gold hunters after their visit to the Mouache Ute, and it was healing well, but a dip in the hot mineral springs of the mountains offered a special comfort and additional healing. The many mountain mineral springs were slowly becoming known as a healing and curative water if for no other reason than the warmth offered in the cool climate of the mountains. The springs were just one of the reasons for their journey of exploration of the valley and nearby settlements.

To the north lay the land of the recent gold strike known as the Pikes Peak Gold Rush. Most of the finds were in an area known as South Park, but with so many gold hunters, most claims had already been staked and latecomers were spilling over into the surrounding countryside. The San Luis Valley and the San Juan Mountains seemed to draw most of the settlers that used the Santa Fe Trail, and many of the gold hunters as well. With Reuben and Elly tasked with keeping the peace between the settlers and the natives in the southern part of the state, they were making a reconnoiter of all the land that lay in their jurisdiction.

The hot springs lay in the thickets of aspen and cottonwood at the edge of the dark skirt of pines that fell from the high peaks. Sloping away from the tree line toward the meandering creek in the bottom of the valley, the land bore an abundance of grasses—Indian, buffalo, bunch, and grama. Prickly pear, hedgehog, and cholla cacti showed themselves amongst the sage and grease-wood. It was true plains and prairie land, but where there was water, green was abundant and colored the flats with bunches of flowers and berry bushes. And while the plains and prairie land summoned sheep-herders and ranchers, the grasslands beckoned farmers and settlers, and the mountains and foothills attracted the gold hunters. Yet everywhere were the native peoples that resented the many intruders, and that conflict and its resolution was what required the presence of the deputy marshals, Reuben and Elly Grundy.

They pushed through the piñon and juniper, crossed a grassy shoulder that was bordered by bunches of lupine and penstemon flowers that showed pale blues and faded violet blossoms standing on tall stalks, and faced the wide pool of steaming water. Shallow at the edges, the water showed a deeper turquoise color in the depths, and Elly turned her smiling face to Reuben and hurriedly slipped to the ground. She tossed the reins of her Appy to Reuben and began stripping off her tunic, anxious to get into the warm, soothing waters.

Reuben led the horses and mule to the trees and loos-ened the girths, tethered the animals, and took one of the extra blankets from the pack and with his Henry rifle in hand, he walked back to the pool. Elly had found herself a seat and was up to her neck in the warm water, arms floating to the side as she basked in the warmth. She smiled at Reuben, "Come on in! It's wonderful!" she declared, smiling, and beckoning her man to join her.

"Uh, I think I better keep a lookout in case those Capote decide to join us."

"Oh, they aren't anywhere around, you can come in for a while. Leave the rifle within reach and join me." She was smiling and giving him the come-on as she curled her finger to him to draw him closer.

He chuckled, did a walk around and looked everywhere possible, even using the binoculars for a sweeping look-see, and satisfied, he leaned the rifle against a big flat rock at water's edge and began stripping off his buckskins. As he did, Bear splashed into the water, paddling his way to Elly and some attention. She laughed, giggled, and rubbed his head, motioned him to get out and away and the big dog begrudgingly obeyed, but gave a good shake that splashed on both Reuben and Elly, causing them to close their eyes and duck away. When the dog was finished with his shake, Reuben pushed through the waters to join Elly on the moss-covered shelf where she sat comfortably and smiling. Elly frowned at Bear, "You keep watch now, y'hear?" she ordered, pointing her finger at the big dog. He had turned around, dropped to his belly, and was facing her as she barked her order. Bear lifted his head, opened his big mouth to let his long tongue loll out, and appeared to nod his head in understanding, dropping it to his paws to watch the bathers rather than the surrounding hillsides.

It was about an hour later when the two emerged, bodies red from the heat and laughing at one another for their resemblance to boiled lobsters, although neither had ever seen a boiled lobster. They quickly dried off with the blanket and were soon mounted up and back on the trail, refreshed, but somewhat drained, for the warm mineral waters, although refreshing, seemed to take something out of a person. They had traveled a short distance when Reuben looked to Elly and pointed to another cluster of aspen, "How 'bout we take a noonin' in the trees yonder. I'll go to the creek, see if I can get us some trout, and we can have some fish and cornbread for lunch."

Elly smiled, "Oh sure, you get to go fishing and I have to do the cooking!" she pouted, and made as if she was mad, but laughed as she added, "Oh, go ahead. I'm no good at fishing anyway, at least not the way you do it!"

"That's alright, you won't be complainin' when I bring back some tasty trout!" declared Reuben, grinning and laughing as he started for the creek below.

Elly turned back to the clearing among the aspen. They had always been careful in their choices of campsites, even those for midday meals or breaks, and this site was in the midst of a thicket of aspen with scrub oak heavy above them and willows surrounding the small spring below them. Elly made a small ring of rocks for the fire, beneath the outstretched limbs of the big aspen. With the small hat-sized fire started, she stepped back to check the rising smoke, making certain the limbs and leaves of the aspen dissipated the wispy column of smoke. Satisfied, she grabbed up the coffeepot and started to the spring for some fresh water, paused and frowned, and went to the gear to get Reuben's binoculars. She hung them around her neck and started through the trees. The horses had been tethered in the trees within reach of graze and they had been given ample water before Reuben left, now they stood, heads down, enjoying the early summer greenery.

The creek in the bottom of the valley, a little over a mile below their camp, meandered through the thick willows, leaving backwater sloughs that bore thick stands of cattails. But what Reuben appreciated most was the many undercut banks at every bend in the creek. He was not fishing for fun; this was for food and he remembered the time when his father first taught him about fishing for food. He said, "Son, there are times when we'll use a pole and a line to do the fishing, that's when we're goin' fishin' in the lakes or ponds or just fishin' for fun. But when we're fishin' for food and we gotta have it, this is how it's done!" His pa had bellied down in the grass on the edge of the bank, reached over the edge and felt around in the water in the undercut. He motioned to his young son, and as he bellied down beside him, he whispered, "You hafta cup your hand, slowly feel around just like you're another fish. And when you feel one, slide your hand up underneath, slowly close it and real quick-like, slide your hand up to the gills and…" and he snatched up a nice trout and rolled over, trout in hand and dropped it on the grass, grinning at his amazed son.

Reuben let a smile cut his face as he walked to the bank of the creek, pushing aside the willows to work his way closer to the grassy bank. He was focused on the creek but had one of those chills run up his spine and he dropped to a crouch and looked all around, spotting some riders coming up along the far side of the creek, staying well away from the willows. He slowly moved back into the willows, his Henry cradled in his arms at his chest, lowering himself into the thicket just enough to provide cover, but still able to see into the valley.

Bear walked before Elly, tail wagging, tongue lolling, his pace making it look like he was bouncing through the tall grass. Elly watched him, enjoying his jaunty manner, but the dog suddenly stopped, dropped his head into his attack stance, shoulders high, one paw lifted and a growl giving warning. Elly froze, looked where Bear's eyes were focused, and saw riders in the valley below, about where Reuben had been bound. She dropped the coffeepot, lifted the binoculars as she went to one knee. Using her knee to support an elbow, she searched the valley bottom for Reuben, but not seeing him, she focused on the riders. Ute!

As she scanned the party, she recognized one of the riders as a white man, the others were Ute, the same bunch they had encountered before. Although she remembered Reuben telling White Skunk that he would shoot the hat off the white man, they had not discussed the presence of a white man with a war party. She frowned as she kept the field glasses on the riders, then moved them back to search the willows and creek bank for Reuben. She knew his habit was to belly down and hand fish, yet she hoped he had seen the war party and taken cover. She uttered a quick prayer to keep him away from the Ute and continued her scan. There! In the willows! She saw the familiar figure of her man in a deep thicket of willows, staying low and out of sight. She breathed a sigh of relief and lifted the binoculars to the war party.

5 / PASS

The war party moved slowly, horses at a steady walk, as the men talked. The leader, White Skunk, rode beside the white man and both talked animatedly. The entire band pulled into a break of the willows just below Reuben to give their horses a drink, but they were too far for him to hear everything, but the bits and pieces he did hear, he did not like. The white man, who White Skunk called Bear Face, which made Reuben chuckle because it was a description that fit the big man with thick black whiskers, often pointed at White Skunk and spoke of gold, but the leader ended the conversation with an adamant, "Navukihkay!" which Reuben recognized as "We will go to war!"

Although it seemed longer to Reuben as he stayed unmoving in the willows, it was just a few moments before the war party moved on, passing by Reuben's position in the thickets and continuing upstream along the meandering creek. Reuben came from the willows, turned toward the camp to see if it was visible, and satisfied, resumed his fishing. It took him just a short while to land four nice-sized brook trout, quickly gutted them and started back to the trees to the waiting Elly.

"Did you see..." he began.

But a somber Elly nodded and said, "Yes, I saw them. I was scared for you, but I saw you in the willows and knew you had seen them. I watched until they were well away from you and saw they were probably heading over the pass, the same way we're goin'!"

"Then I reckon we'll just hafta be extra cautious! I wanna go down the pass, see if we can find that fella that was settin' up a tradin' post and find out what's been happenin' in the valley down yonder. That area appears to be a crossroads of folks comin' over from South Pass and Breckenridge and California Gulch. I guess it's the Arkansas River that draws 'em."

As the sun dropped over the San Juans, Reuben and Elly crested the mountain pass known as Poncha Pass. "The commandant at Fort Garland said this pass was first crossed in 1779 by a Spanish expedition led by Juan Bautista de Anza. And the First Cavalry Regiment under Colonel Thomas Fauntleroy chased some Utes over this pass about a decade ago, so the Utes have been fightin' newcomers for some time!" declared Reuben as he nudged Blue into the trees. The thick pines and firs parted briefly to allow the two into the small clearing, offering shelter and cover. "And since we haven't crossed the trail of that war party, I'm thinkin' they turned into the western mountains, maybe goin' into the San Juans."

"I hope so!" answered Elly as she slipped to the ground. As Reuben alighted, she tossed the reins of her Appy to him and went to the pack mule to start unloading their gear and cooking utensils. Reuben tended to the horses, stripping the gear, and letting them roll before taking the mule from Elly and stripping off the packs and saddle from the weary burden-bearer. He began giving all of them a rubdown with handfuls of grass and led them down to the little creek that sided the trail. When they were satisfied, they returned to the camp and Reuben picketed them within reach of the grass but still in the trees.

Elly said, "You wanna fill the coffeepot?"

"Sure, I can do that!" he answered, noticing she already had a fire going and strips of meat sizzling over the flames as she worked preparing some cornmeal biscuits and more.

When he returned, he sat the coffeepot near the flames and offered to help, but she smiled and answered, "No need, I'm just about finished."

As dusk was dropping its curtain of darkness, Bear came to his feet when he heard the chorus of wolves somewhere high up, probably about timberline, as they began their mournful howls that carried across the narrow pass and down into the wide valley. Bear looked back to Elly, turned back to the direction of the howls, and danced about as if he wanted to join the mountain choir. But he remained in camp, staying close to Elly, showing a little more concern for her protection than usual.

As the wolves fell silent, the void was filled by the buzzing racketing of mountain cicadas, a rattling sound that is almost mesmerizing and somewhat hypnotic. Reuben looked at Elly, grinned, "And another chorus sounds! Think that'll put you to sleep?"

"Hope so, course I'd rather have the chuckling sound of a stream nearby, but that's alright."

The trill and chirp of the red-winged blackbird added color to the night as the two lay on their blankets, hands behind their heads as they watched the stars light their lanterns. The black velvet sky began to glisten and sparkle for there were no clouds to dim the glows and the night winds whispered through the pines, carrying the pungent but pleasant smell of pine through the camp. They held hands and prayed together, asking for the Lord's guidance and protection as they carried out their duties in this amazing part of God's wonderful creation. They drifted off to sleep, hand in hand.

At first light, Reuben mounted the bit of a hill behind their camp and spent his usual time with his Lord, reading the Bible and praying. The sun made a dark shadow of the mountains off his right shoulder, painting the eastern horizon as a black jagged line. He returned to camp, wending his way through the close growing aspen, and was greeted by a smiling Elly, a steaming cup of coffee in hand. "As soon as you get the animals rigged, we'll be ready to go!"

They pushed through the thickets of aspen, returned to the well-used trail, and started down the gentle slope that followed the natural contours of the foothills. With the slopes on the right thickly forested with pine and juniper, those on the left were sprinkled with juniper and piñon while sparse willows and alders sided the now shallow runoff creek beds in the bottom. As the trail bent to the north, the hills pushed back and offered a glimpse of the distant Arkansas River Valley about five miles away.

When they broke from the hills, the wide green valley before them lay at the base of the Sawatch Range that bordered the long valley on the west. With granite-tipped peaks, the range held many mountains that topped fourteen thousand feet and stood proudly with their bald heads in the blue sky as they marched northward. Their black skirts of thick timber blanketed the foothills below them and tapered off to grassy, dry plains that offered bunchgrass, gramma, and Indian grass, amongst the sage, greasewood, and a variety of cacti.

The trail they had traveled was sided by the small Poncha Creek that was continually added to by the many runoff creeks in the foothills, but the creek fed the South Fork of the Arkansas River as it entered the wide valley. As the river flowed eastward, Reuben and Elly crossed the narrow river, and stopped to look around at what appeared to be the beginning of a settlement. The cottonwoods gave way to some burr oak and hackberry that sheltered a few recently built log cabins. Standing on the stoop of one, and watching the two newcomers, was a woman in a long gingham dress, an apron around her waist, and hand shading her eyes as she gave them the once-over.

When she recognized one of the riders as a woman, the settler called out, "Welcome! Come on over!" as she waved at the couple.

Reuben chuckled as Elly looked at him, smiling, "Guess she's wantin' comp'ny, ya' s'pose?" she said, nudging her mare toward the cabin.

As they neared, the smiling woman said, "I'm Maribel Rich, my husband, Nat, is out in the woods, hunting, but he'll be back soon. Light a spell and we'll have some coffee!" she declared, wringing her hands in her apron, and smiling. "I declare, I haven't had a woman to talk to in I don't know how long, seems to me to be nigh on to six months or more, mercy me!" As she watched Elly and Reuben step down to tie the animals to the hitchrail near the water trough, she continued to talk excitedly and continually until Elly stepped up on the stoop beside her and she declared, "Why, you're just a little whip of a girl, and young and pretty too! Whatever are you doing out here in the wilderness all by your lonesome?!" But without waiting for a response, the woman continued, "Come on now, let's get us some coffee!" and turned into the doorway and led the way into the comfortable log home.

As she puttered about the counter, fetching coffee cups and snatching the coffeepot from the swivel hook at the fireplace, she talked incessantly. "It was us an' the Hendricks, Bob and his wife Susan, that were the first to build cabins here. Oh, 'fore we got here there were others, but none what stayed on, and this spring, John and Minerva Maxwell Burnett joined us. They're buildin' them a cabin back in the trees alongside the river yonder. Ain't very many of us, but there's more comin', what with the gold strike up in South Park gettin' too crowded and us gettin' the overflow!" She paused as she poured the coffee, looked directly at Elly, "You folks gonna be settlin' down? You know at your age, it's 'bout time to put down some roots! That's what we done," she stood and patted her tummy, smiled, "an' we're gonna add to the family come early spring!"

"Oh! You're going to have a baby?" asked Elly, leaning forward over the edge of the table, eyes wide and looking at Maribel who had finally seated herself.

Her head nodding and her smile spreading, she answered, "Indeed I am." She paused, her hand on her apron, "But we don't have a midwife or doctor or nuthin' hereabouts an'…could you do the midwifin'?"

Elly looked from Maribel to Reuben and back again, cocking her head to the side, "Well, I tell you what, Maribel, if we're anywhere nearabouts, I'd be happy to stop by and see if I can be of help. I haven't done it all, but I've helped before so..." as she shrugged and smiled.

"Oh, that'd be fine! Just fine!" answered Maribel, a smile showing her obvious relief. "If you folks would like, you could sleep in the lean-to. It's not much, but it's better'n nuthin'!"

Elly looked at Reuben and he spoke up, "I think we'll get us a camp back in the trees yonder, near the river. We might be around a few days, I'd like to talk to your man and the neighbors, see how things have been." He looked at Maribel, "Have you folks had any trouble with the natives?"

Maribel's face sobered as she frowned, "No! No! We haven't! But I've heard about some problems. Nat knows more'n I do, and he should be back soon, but I don't think it was much."

Reuben looked to Elly, "If you wanna stay and visit, I'll find us a place to camp and come back, if you'd like?"

Elly nodded, smiling, "That'd be fine, Reuben. If you don't mind?"

Reuben nodded, stood, and with a tip of his hat to the ladies, walked out to the horses.

6 / NEWS

They had made camp in a little parklike setting beside the South Fork of the Arkansas River and rose early the next morning. To greet the rising sun and spend his time with his Lord, Reuben went to the top of the hill that lay just south of the river and was sprinkled with piñon and juniper and stood like the last sentinel of a long ridge, one of many that appeared as folds in the wrinkled skirt of ridges that flanked the high foothills. From the crest of the hill, he could see back up the long canyon of Poncha Creek, where they traveled from the San Luis Valley, and survey the wide flats of the Arkansas River that lay below the foothills on the east and before the long line of snowcapped peaks of the Sawatch Range. But he also got the lay of the land where the new cabins were rising at the confluence of Poncha Creek and the South Arkansas River.

The cottonwoods, alders, burr oak, and hackberry, were thick along the banks of the little river, offering shade and cover to the new settlers, yet the cleared patches that held the new cabins showed as a patchwork quilt. He scanned the valley with his binoculars, saw a little activity to the east, close to the mouth of the narrow canyon of the Arkansas, a few deer upstream on the little river, and in the distance, he was certain he saw a small herd of elk. But this early in the morning with the sun yet to show its face yet laying out the blanket of early morning light, he did not expect to see much activity, at least not of the two-legged variety. He finished his look-see and picked up his rifle, Bible, and binoculars and with Bear at his heels, he started down the angled trail to make his way back to camp.

He was greeted with a surprise breakfast as Elly knelt, smiling, and tending the frying pan that held three nice-sized duck eggs, sizzling in the bacon grease. Reuben took a deep breath of the smell of breakfast, a wide grin splitting his face and went to his woman, bent down behind her, and nuzzled her neck as he whispered, "I love you!"

"Oh, you're just saying that 'cuz you're hungry!" chuckled Elly, turning to smile at her man.

"Well—" he laughed and went to the packs for the tin plates and cups. The coffee was smelling good, and he was anxious to get started. They made short work of the breakfast, enjoying not just the meal but the time together. Although they were almost never apart, their times together were always treasured and appreciated. As they sat back to enjoy the second cup of coffee, Elly asked, "So, are we goin' to the barn raisin'?"

"Sure! That would be a great time to get to know the folks and to find out what's been going on in the area. If the men can't say, I'm sure Maribel would be glad to fill us in on all the happenin's!"

"Wouldn't she, though," giggled Elly, smiling at the remembrance, "That woman certainly keeps her eyes and ears open as to whatever is going on anywhere!"

"But she means well," added Reuben, sipping on his coffee. "But we best be gettin' a move on or they'll have the barn raised and we'll miss out on all the work!"

Elly giggled, shaking her head, and tossed out the dregs of her coffee and rose to finish the cleanup while Reuben saddled the horses and readied their gear. They would leave the mule in camp, picketed within reach of water and graze, and knew he would enjoy the day of rest. They soon mounted up and started across the shallow waters to make their way to the work site.

It did not take long for the small group to assemble at the site of the Burnetts' cabin. It was to be more than a barn raising, for the cabin was in need of a roof and the couple stood by their wagon, greeting everyone as they arrived. As Reuben and Elly rode up, the couple smiled and greeted them, "Oh, you must be the couple that Maribel spoke about. It is good to have you with us today, we need all the help we can get." It was Minerva that was the talkative one of the couple and John simply nodded his head and extended his hand to shake as Reuben stepped down for the introductions.

After shaking John's hand, he nodded to Minerva, "Mrs. Burnett, let me introduce my wife, Elly," motioning to Elly to come close, "and I'm Reuben Grundy, the proud husband of this little filly!" he chuckled as he looked at his little woman, who smiled and greeted the couple. Minerva sort of cornered Elly and drew her away from the men, prompting the men to walk side by side toward the stack of peeled logs that would be used as the rafters for the roof.

John asked, "You built any log cabins before, Reuben?"

Reuben nodded, "We built us a cabin up in the valley below the Sangres last summer."

"Oh!?" responded John, surprised at the young man having already built a cabin and spent time in the mountains.

Reuben chuckled, "Yeah, Elly's not one for sleepin' outside in the wintertime."

"Can't say as I blame her. It does get cold up in the high country and we get a lot o' that white stuff that doesn't help either."

As John sorted through the lodgepole pine logs, Reuben asked, "So, Maribel said you were thinkin' about putting in a trading post?"

"Ummhmm. Governor Evans, who was also the superintendent of Indian Affairs, had asked me to serve as an Indian Agent to the Southern Ute, the Capote, Mouache, and Tabeguache, and I thought by having a trading post, it would make it easier to distribute the annuities and such."

"And how's that going so far?" asked Reuben, frowning.

"Not so good. I've only met a handful of Capote and I think they were more renegade than friendly. None of 'em seemed to be a chief, but there was one that spoke for the others, White Skunk."

"Ummhmm, met him. The treaty with the Tabeguache and the others, the one that ceded all the San Luis Valley, that ever get ratified?"

Burnett frowned and turned to look at Reuben, "You seem to know a lot about the happenings in the area."

"A little, so, was it? Ratified, I mean."

"Not yet, and I think it'll probably go the way of most of the other treaties and end up on some politician's desk gatherin' dust!" answered Burnett, his contempt showing. "Don't know how they expect me to accomplish anything when they don't know what they want done! That's one o' the reasons I thought it best to put in a trading post."

"When you met with White Skunk, friendly?"

"No. He was a little intimidating, what with the warriors with him and just me'n the missus. But when I told him I was to be the agent and would be responsible for the annuities, he backed off a little. Grunted mostly, shook his weapon at me as they turned to leave and they left in a hurry, too."

"You know anything about a white man that rides with 'em?"

"A white man?"

"Ummhmm. Big man, face full of black whiskers, and I'm guessin' he's with 'em to scout out some country for gold diggins."

"You know, there was a man that fit that description that came through here a little over a week ago, he was with a couple other scruffy lookin' men. They didn't stay long, just kinda looked the place over, saw 'em tryin' a few pans in the river yonder, then they just rode off up the canyon yonder," pointing to the trail that led to Poncha Pass. "Truth be told, we were a little relieved to see 'em ride off. There ain't that many of us," as he spoke, he looked toward the cabin to see several others had arrived and four other men were walking toward them. He grinned and looked from the new arrivals to Reuben, "Here they are now." He looked back at the men, smiling and nodding, "Men, come meet our visitor."

As they neared, Burnett began introducing, "Men, this is Reuben Grundy, the husband of that little bit of a blonde woman with my wife. Reuben, this is Nat Rich, husband of Maribel whom you already met. And this is Bob Hendricks, Joe Hutchinson, and John McPherson."

As he spoke each man's name, they stepped forward and shook Reuben's hand and made token greetings.

Nat Rich looked to Burnett, "Well, looks like the first thing we need to get started on is your roof. These the logs for the rafters?"

"That's right, and that bigger one yonder," pointing to a log that lay beside the cabin wall, "is the ridge beam and as you know, we'll need to get that up first!"

The men set to and worked well together. Conversation was secondary to the work and each man found his place in the work crew and within a couple hours, the ridge beam and rafters were in place and the men agreed it was time for coffee. The women had the coffee on but had commandeered the table and chairs forcing the men to take their coffee to the shady side of the cabin and be seated on a couple of leftover logs.

Nat Rich looked to Reuben, "So, you and your lady gonna be settlin' down around here?"

Reuben shook his head, looked up at Nat and answered, "No, we're just scoutin' out the territory. We have a cabin up in what's called the Wet Mountain Valley."

The curiosity of settlers regarding any newcomer always tugs at their minds but in the west, it was considered ill-mannered to ask too much of another. But Bob Hendricks was never one to be too concerned with formalities or customs and after taking a sip of the hot brew, he looked to Reuben, "So, scoutin'? Any special reason?"

Reuben grinned, "You might say that. My wife and I have been tasked with trying to keep the peace between the native peoples and settlers and gold hunters that want to take over the San Luis Valley."

The men frowned, lowered their cups, and looked at

the man before them. Reuben grinned, "You see, we are deputy marshals, and the task was given to us by the Western District Marshal, Theodore Moses and the territory marshal, Uriah Holloway. Of course, we were first appointed by Governor Evans at the request of Ben Holladay."

"Hold on there. You mean to say that you *and* your wife are both marshals?" asked Bob Hendricks, glancing around the group of men, all of whom showed the same question on their faces.

Reuben grinned, "That's right. You see, when Holladay first wanted me as a marshal, I told him me and my wife are always together and I wouldn't be goin' anywhere without her, and since she can shoot just as good as I can, he thought it'd be a good idea for her to have a badge, too, and the district marshal, Moses, agreed."

"Ain't never heard of such a thing!" declared Hendricks, shaking his head, and looking around. "What's a little bit of a woman like her goin' to do anyway?" he asked, looking back to Reuben.

"Just don't let her hear you talk like that. I've seen her take down men bigger'n you and she can shoot straighter and faster than most men I've known. And I've known a few since I was part of Berdan's Sharpshooters in the war."

The men's faces seemed to melt at Reuben's remark, and they sat silent for a few moments, pondering the thought of a woman marshal. As they sipped their coffee and contemplated, Reuben asked, "Any of you folks have any trouble with the natives or the gold hunters hereabouts?"

Burnett spoke up, "Not that I know of, Marshal, only

what we already talked about." As he spoke, he looked at the other men who nodded in agreement.

"Well, I think White Skunk, the leader of that band of renegades, is trying to recruit other malcontents and he has at least one white man that's tryin' to get the location of gold out of him." Reuben looked at Burnett, "I don't know if you noticed the gold nugget that White Skunk had in the middle of his breastplate. But the white man with him certainly did and I think they might be workin' together toward that end. So, you might want to stay prepared. They tried to take a wagon and such from a family earlier this week, but we discouraged them, but I think they might try to bully other settlers and gold hunters. As far as I know, they'll prob'ly stay in the San Luis Valley, but you can never tell about them."

"Have you had much to do with the natives, Marshal?" asked McPherson.

Reuben chuckled, "You might say that. The Pawnee, Sioux, Arapaho, Cheyenne, Kiowa, Mouache, Tabeguache, and Capote Ute. Most recently, Chief Kaniache of the Mouache."

7 / TROUBLE

"I ain't lyin' to ya! That's what I heard that grumpy ol' goat tell his woman! That fella what was buildin' his cabin's gonna be an Injun agent and he's settin' him up a tradin' post. That's what fer he's got him two wagons! That other'ns the one with all the trade goods and such," declared the tall, lanky, freckle-faced redhead. He was the junior member of the group of renegades who called him Freckles, although his name was Louis Franklin and he hailed from the hills of Kentucky.

"Wal, if'n he's got all that, what're we waitin' fer? We can just go in there an' *take* what we want. He don't look like he could find his way outta no cornfield an'd prob'ly scare himself to death if'n he could!" whined Pork, the shortest one of the trio whose name was Ed Przyzycki. He had earned his nickname by his stature which held an uncanny resemblance to a bovine. He was built like a barrel, had ham hocks for hands, thin hair, and a nose that poked from his splotched face and showed wide nostrils resembling a sizable pig. He prided himself in his fighting ability, often choosing to beat a man to death rather than waste a bullet, usually ending up with more blood of his opponent on him than his own.

It was out of the ordinary for the two of them to be on their own, having been recruited by the bigger man, Horace Hickam, who had joined the renegade Utes led by White Skunk and had summarily dispatched the two to find supplies for their current search for gold. They sat just inside the tree line, astride their mounts, Freckles on his spavined bay horse and his legs so long his feet hung below the horse's belly, and Pork aboard his dark grey mule. While Freckles resembled his bony old horse, Pork looked like a big ball balanced atop his recalcitrant mule. They watched as the villagers worked on the roof of the cabin and were called to eat by the wives who had been busy preparing the midday meal as they talked about their men.

Pork looked at Freckles, "Shore would like to sit down at that meal with 'em, and maybe have one o' them women fer dessert!"

"The only dessert you'd get is a rear end full o' buckshot were you to invite yo'sef to their doins! We'll just wait till we can get that agent feller alone, an' we'll knock him out or put yore sticker twixt his ribs and take all we want. He has him a purty good hoss in that there corral an' we can use one o' them mules fer packin' the goods whut we take! But fer now, how 'bout we get back in these hyar trees an' take us a nap?"

"I'm fer that. If'n I can sleep what with yore belly grumblin' all the while!"

"Ah, we can take our fill on them thar leftovers after ever'body leaves out!"

Had anyone been listening to the two, they would have easily mistaken their voices as to who was talking. While the tall, lanky Freckles had a deep bass voice, low and broad, Pork had a high-pitched voice that grated as if coming from the rafters. The two had been companions since long before teaming up with Bear Face, as the Utes called him, and were loyal to one another although they fought and bickered continually, with Pork usually condescending to the ways of his thin friend. He often kidded Freckles, "Why, you're so skinny, when you turn sideways you have to stick out yore tongue to cast a shadow!" To which Freckles usually responded, "An' if'n you was to put yore tongue back in yore face, you'd roll downhill like a ball!"

Nat Rich and Bob Hendricks spent most of the day sawing logs into planks, the other men were busy with finishing the roof of the cabin, using the planks to overlap and with a sealant of adobe and grass between the edges, they made a weathertight roof. Nat and Bob had lost the coin toss and would alternate positions on the cutting frame with one on top to draw the saw up and the other man below, pulling down on the two-man saw as it ripped through the logs, each cut making a plank. John McPherson had a forge in his barn that he used to craft the square nails used to secure the planks to the log rafters.

The villagers worked well together, and all were appreciative of the help from both Reuben and Elly as they pitched in to work with the men and women at the various tasks. The men often questioned Reuben about his duties and work as a marshal to which Reuben was hesitant to talk about but shared enough with them to satisfy their curiosity as to if the young couple could provide the help they might need in a time of trouble.

"So, are you'ns gonna be hereabouts very long?" asked Joe Hutchinson.

"Oh, we'll be around this part for a while yet, but if

we're needed, you can always get word to us through Fort Garland. It's a big territory and our responsibility is for the southern part, but most folks, both native and others, will know us and we won't be that difficult to find."

"I just can't get used to the idea of a woman bein' a deputy marshal!" declared John Burnett. "But times are changin', but if'n my wife was to be a deputy, the most dangerous part about her is her waggin' tongue and shakin' finger!" he chuckled as he mimicked his wife shaking her finger at him.

"Well, if my wife is shaking her finger at you, you best watch out, because it's probably on the trigger of her pistol!" added Reuben, chuckling.

The repartee of the men continued, with most of the talk about their hopes and dreams for their futures, farming, and ranching and more, while the women spoke of things domestic. It was Susan Hendricks that asked, "So, how did the two of you meet?"

Elly smiled at the memory and began to relate, "My father had converted to Mormonism so we could join the wagon train heading west, but my mom and I weren't so convinced, but we made friends among the others. And when we were coming west, a Sioux war party attacked our wagon train, took several of us girls captive and were taking us back to their village, when this tall, good-looking blonde man come along and rescued us!" She chuckled at the response of the women who were alarmed at learning she had been captured by the natives, but laughed when she described her rescuer. "So, I guess you could call it love at first sight, because he followed us and told me he wanted me to be his wife and we were married by Little Raven, a chief of the Arapaho nation!" The women were giddy as they chattered, asking Elly many questions and the more she told, the more they wanted to hear.

As the day drew to a close, the men weary, the women tired but refreshed, they left with cheerful good-byes and parted to their separate ways. Reuben and Elly geared up their horses in the corral and led them out, mounted, and started for their camp in the trees near the river. As they neared their camp, Bear stopped, growling, and searching the trees west of the clearing. Reuben and Elly stopped, watching the dog, and looking through the thicket of cottonwood and alders. They saw nothing, but both heard horses moving through the trees. At Reuben's signal, they pushed through the trees toward the sounds, thinking there was something amiss about horses in the trees away from the usual trails.

As they neared the tree line, they saw two riders moving toward the Burnett cabin. The couple were making ready to spend the first night in their cabin with the new roof and were carrying bedding and more into their new abode. As they approached the doorway, they were hailed by the two renegades that rode into the clearing.

"Ho, the cabin! Can we come in?" called Freckles, one hand lifted in greeting.

John Burnett turned to face them; his arms full of goods for their cabin. "C'mon in if you're friendly!" he answered, and continued, "Let me put this stuff away and I'll be right back out. Go ahead and step down. You can water your horses at the trough," nodding toward the long water trough near the corral, "if you're of a mind to!"

Freckles nodded and swung his leg over the rump of his horse, grinning at Pork when his back was turned to the cabin. Pork followed suit and crooked his leg over the pommel and slid to the ground beside his mule. They led the horses to the trough, unfastening their coats to expose their pistols stuffed in their belts. Freckles glanced back to the door, turned back to Pork, and spoke softly, "I'll walk up close to the man, get the drop on him, an' you can go in the cabin fer the woman."

Pork grinned, chuckling, and rubbing his palms together, "Best idee I heerd all day!"

Reuben looked at Elly, "You work your way through the trees, beyond the corral, and see if you can come up on the backside of the cabin. I don't like the looks of this, and I think they're up to no good. I'll give you some time, take Bear with you, and then I'll confront them here in the clearing before the cabin."

Elly looked at Reuben, "Be careful, I don't like this either." She nudged her Appy and pushed through the trees to work around the corral and lean-to. With a glance over her shoulder, she disappeared into the thicket. Reuben watched the two men separate, saw the lanky one slap the rein of his mount over the rail fence and start toward the cabin. Reuben noticed the man checking his pistol before he approached the door just as John Burnett opened the door to see the men.

Reuben stepped down, dropped the reins to ground tie Blue, and with his Henry rifle in hand, he started into the clearing, using the two wagons for cover. As he neared, he saw the pistol in the lanky one's hand and watched as he waved the pistol toward the wagons, making Burnett move as he directed. Reuben stepped to the far side of the second wagon, watching around the corner of the bonnet as the two men approached. Reuben moved as they drew near, always keeping the wagon between them. As Burnett and Freckles approached, Reuben moved behind the lanky man as

Freckles demanded, "Pull that bonnet aside, I wanna see what'chu got in thar!"

Burnett reached for the hanging tarp that covered the rear opening of the wagon, started drawing it aside just as Reuben stuck the barrel of the Henry in Freckles's ribs and spoke softly but demanding, "Lift 'em!"

Freckles started to turn but Reuben jammed the Henry into his ribs, making him wince and stagger as Reuben said, "Drop that pistol NOW!"

Freckles complied and started pleading, "Now don't go getting' anxious there. I din't mean him no harm, just wanted to see what he had!"

"Ummhmmm, just wanted to see what you could steal, you mean."

Freckles started to turn, but Reuben stopped him with another jab to the ribs, "Don't move! John, get somethin' to tie him up with."

Burnett reached into the bed of the wagon and brought out a length of rope. He cut off a short piece, turned and grabbed one of Freckles's hands and wrapped a loop of the rope around it, then grabbed the other and soon had the feckless robber tied and stuffed a rag in his mouth to keep him silent. Burnett looked at Reuben, "There were two of 'em! Where's the other'n?"

"I think he went into your cabin after your wife, but he's in for a surprise."

The men looked toward the cabin to see the fat man come out with hands held high and a Henry rifle behind him. A smiling Elly looked at Reuben and poked the would-be outlaw in the ribs to force him toward the others. A chuckling Burnett grabbed another length of rope and soon had the second man secured. Reuben said, "Alright, turn back-to-back and sit down!"

The men complied and were sitting back-to-back,

leaning against one another as John wrapped a long length of rope around the pair and tied it tight. He shook his head as he looked to Reuben, “I sure am grateful you were here! I think they planned to steal all my goods and I don’t know what all!”

“I know what all!” declared a fidgety Minerva Burnett as she stood beside Elly, her hands on her hips as she glowered at the men. She turned to Elly, “Would you teach me how to shoot a gun? I’ve been after that man,” nodding toward her husband, “but he says I don’t need to know how! Well, this proves my point! If you’ns weren’t here, that fat bum woulda had his way with me an’ I could’na done nuthin’ ‘bout it!”

8 / RESOLUTION

"So, what are we gonna do with 'em?" asked John Burnett, looking at Reuben and Elly who stood looking at the two bound outlaws who continually fussed with one another over their botched robbery.

"Well, since you don't have a jail, and I'm not about to take 'em all the way to Fort Garland, I guess it's up to you. I s'pose you could have a trial among the villagers, and then maybe use 'em as convict labor to help you finish buildin' your place. Or, maybe do like they do on a ship, give 'em forty lashes with a bullwhip and let 'em loose," suggested Reuben, removing his hat and scratching his head.

"But by now, everyone's gone back to their cabins and are fixin' to go to bed!" pleaded Burnett. "They're your prisoners and you're the marshal, so I think it's up to you."

Reuben looked around, turned back to Burnett, "That shed yonder, you said it was to store your goods. Is there any room in there?"

"It's empty! We weren't gonna unload the wagon till after we got the cabin up and moved in, then we would empty that second wagon. The only reason that shed's done is cuz some trapper or somebody used it as a cabin and left the country."

"Then let's lock 'em in there. Let 'em use their own bedrolls, just make sure there's nothing in them, and when the villagers come back tomorrow to help you finish your barn, we'll have a trial and you can decide then whether they get lashes or labor," chuckled Reuben, watching the response of the prisoners to the expression 'lashes.'

"That sounds good to me. I'll check the shed and door, make sure they're safe, and you can bring those two and we'll lock 'em up."

Reuben nodded, turned to Elly, "You get their bedrolls and I'll get them on their feet." Elly nodded and went to the men's horses while Reuben stepped closer to the two bound prisoners. He grabbed the arms of the men and helped them to their feet while they complained and whined. "If you don't hush, I'll let you stay bound together for the night and see how much sleep you get. Behave yourselves and you can have your bedrolls and stretch out."

"Are you really a marshal?" asked Freckles, the two men sidestepping toward the shed.

"That's right, I'm one of two marshals for the southern territory."

"Who's the other'n?"

"My wife," answered Reuben, nodding toward Elly as she followed with the bedrolls.

"Yore wife? Ain't no woman no marshal!" declared Pork.

Elly laughed, "You just try somethin' and you'll see a marshal that's all woman show you how she can shoot and make you dance like a frog on a hot rock!"

"But, Marshal, we ain't done nothin' so why you got us all tied up an' such?" whined Pork.

"It's what you tried to do! Your partner had Burnett under the gun and wanted to steal his trade goods and you! You were in the cabin and my partner there, you know, the woman that can't be a marshal? I don't know what all happened, but I saw you comin' from the cabin lookin' like a hog goin' to slaughter with your hands raised high."

"But, we didn't *do* nuthin'! You can't arrest us just for thinkin' about it!"

"Looks to me like we did!" replied Reuben, chuckling as he looked at his smiling wife. Elly had gone into the shed and rolled out the bedrolls to make sure there were no hidden weapons, stood and went to the doorway.

"We sure did!" declared a grinning Elly. "And if you *think* about doing anything else, there's no limit to what we may do to you. Who knows, maybe we'll haul you out in the middle of that river and make you serve your sentence in the cold water!"

"Ah come on! You wouldn't do that to a feller?"

"Try us and see!" declared Reuben, with one eyebrow raised and scowling at the two.

IT WAS SHORTLY AFTER FIRST LIGHT WHEN REUBEN RODE into the clearing of Burnett's cabin. He stepped down, ground tied Blue, and went to the cabin. The door that had been secured now stood ajar, the leather hinges cut, and the floor of the cabin held the rope that had bound the two outlaws. Reuben snatched up the rope, saw it had been cut, and realized the two must have had a hideout knife used to make their escape. As he came from the shed, he looked about, walked to the corral, and saw only the seven mules of Burnett, but also saw the spavined horse that had been ridden by the lanky outlaw called Freckles. The buckskin gelding of Burnett was gone as was the mule ridden by Pork. Reuben shook his head and began searching for tracks of the escapees' horses, saw the tracks of the horses but the men's tracks were also visible. As he followed the sign, they had apparently gone to the second wagon and taken some of the goods before making their escape. Reuben shook his head and started back to his horse when Burnett came from the cabin.

"What's the matter?" asked Burnett.

"They're gone! Must've had a hidden knife, cut the ropes, and stole your saddle horse, a mule, and some of your goods," nodding back to the cabin, "and lit out. Looks like they're headin' back up Poncha Creek, prob'ly goin' to join up with their partner and the renegade Utes."

"What'cha gonna do?"

"Go after 'em, I reckon. After we've had our breakfast!"

"Well, I'll check to see what they took and let you know 'fore you go."

Reuben nodded and stepped aboard Blue, reined the gelding around to return to camp and his wife and their breakfast. Elly had biscuits baking in the Dutch Oven that sat near the fire, resting on a bed of coals with more coals on the lid. Bacon was crackling in the frying pan and the coffeepot danced beside the fire. Although the tantalizing smells of breakfast were welcome, it was the smile on Elly's face that made Reuben's face split with a grin. He stepped down, tethered Blue to the nearby tree, loosened the girth, and walked to Elly's side. She greeted him with a warm embrace and a lingering kiss, pulled back and asked, "What's wrong?"

Reuben shook his head, "The two outlaws escaped last night. Musta had a knife hid out, maybe in their boot or something, but they cut their bonds and stole Burnett's horse and some of his goods and lit out!"

Elly frowned, turned back to tend to the bacon and looked up as Reuben seated himself on the grey log opposite the fire, "Maybe that's a good thing."

Reuben's brow wrinkled as he cocked his head to the side, showing rather than asking the question.

"Well, they probably had someplace they'd meet up with the other'n. You know, the white man that was with the Ute raiding party?"

Reuben slowly shook his head, letting his expression relax, and said, "So, we can follow 'em, maybe catch all three with the Ute's and…" he shrugged, "and then what? We can't take on the whole raiding party!"

"Well, no, but we might find out what they're up to, no good of course, but at least we'll have a better chance of knowing and that's half the battle."

"Yeah, I s'pose. But for now, I'm hungry!" he grinned as Elly giggled, shaking her head.

THEY BROKE CAMP, GEARED UP, AND HEADED FOR Burnett's cabin. The other villagers were gathering there for another day of building and hoped to finish the barn so they could return to their own homesteads. As Reuben and Elly rode from the trees, they were warmly greeted but Reuben was peppered with questions regarding the outlaws. Burnett had told the villagers about the attempted robbery and escape of the brigands, and they were anxious as to the action of the marshals.

"Are you goin' after 'em now?" asked one.

"What're ya' gonna do?" asked another.

"Can't let 'em get away! They need to be locked up, or sumpin'!" declared another.

Reuben had stepped down and now held his hands up, seeking an opportunity to talk. When the couples quieted, "We believe these two are part of the bunch that are with White Skunk and the renegade Utes. We plan on following them, see what they might be planning, and act accordingly," explained Reuben.

"Renegades? You mean there's a band of renegade Injuns?" asked Minerva Burnett, fear painting her face.

"Yes ma'am. We ran into 'em 'fore we came here. Not very many, but the other white man of this little bunch was with 'em." Chatter broke out among the group and Reuben raised his hands for their attention, "I don't think you're in danger here, I believe the white men are wanting the natives to lead them to some gold. Their leader, White Skunk, was wearing a gold nugget on his breastplate and the one they called Bear Face, the white man, was after the gold."

"Does that mean we don't have to worry about them comin' here?" asked Maribel Rich.

"Worry doesn't do anyone any good. My dad used to say, 'Worry is like a rockin' chair. It gives you somethin' to do but you don't get anywhere.' But caution is always a good thing. Just stay prepared, keep your weapons handy, be cautious, always have a plan to get together, and I'm sure you'll be alright."

As the small group chattered among themselves, John Burnett stepped closer and spoke quietly with Reuben. "I said I'd let you know what they took. Near as I could figger, it was mostly staples, you know, flour, sugar, and such. But they also found some trade fusils and some powder and took them, four of 'em."

Reuben nodded, "So, you've got some supplies you can spare? We could use a resupply on flour, sugar, coffee, cornmeal," he paused, glanced back to Elly who nodded, but added nothing.

"Sure, sure. Glad to be of help," began Burnett, starting toward his supply wagon. "Anything else? I've got cartridges for those," pointing to the Henry rifle in the scabbard.

"No, we've supplied at the sutler in Fort Garland, but they were a little low on staples, what with so many settlers comin' into the valley."

As Burnett busied himself digging things out of the wagon and Reuben had all he asked for, Burnett grinned as he passed two cans of peaches to the man. Reuben accepted the proffered goods, smiled when he read the label, and said, "I never thought I'd see these out here!"

Burnett chuckled, "That's the least I could do after all you've done. Enjoy those peaches and when you eat 'em, think of us!"

Reuben chuckled, hefting the cans as he turned to put them in the panniers. Elly frowned at his attempt to obscure them from her, and asked, "What'chu got there?"

"A surprise!" chuckled Reuben as he turned and nodded to Burnett. With a couple long strides, he was beside Blue, stuck his foot in the stirrup and swung aboard. With a wave over his shoulder, the chuckling Reuben led them away from the village to start up the trail to Poncha Pass and the renegades.

9 / SEARCH

The long shadows of early morning had retreated into the trees that lined the banks of the small Poncha Creek. The trail that sided the creek mounted the alluvial fans that had formed over eons of time by the spring runoff from deep snow winters. As the creek wound its way past those same mounds and the many steep-sided foothills, its wandering path reminded Reuben of a lazy snake that could not decide between sunning itself on a hot rock or continuing its search for food.

As usual, Bear led the way and scouted the trail far ahead, ignoring the deer and occasional antelope that came to the creek for their morning drink. Although his appearance often spooked the animals to go bounding up the steep slopes to escape, Bear just paused, watched for a moment, then continued his scout. After a little more than an hour on the southbound trail, a dogleg bend pointed them easterly and up a steeper climb through the aspen and their quaking leaves that rattled in the morning breeze. A bit of a grassy basin at the foot of a large cluster of the white-barked trees harbored a small herd of elk, the big cows lifting their heads toward Bear, but perceived no threat and soon dropped their noses into the tall grass, only occasionally lifting to check on the presence of their gangly and playful calves.

Bear sat down on his haunches to watch the gamboling youngsters and soon heard the clatter of hooves that announced the arrival of Reuben and Elly. Bear turned to look at the couple, but without moving, turned back to watch the fearless elk enjoying their morning graze. But the arrival of the riders caught the attention of the herd cow who bleated her warning prompting the small herd to stretch their long legs and trot into the thicket of aspen and disappear.

"They're beautiful animals, but they remind me of pictures I've seen of the camels of the Far East. Their necks have a similar dip, and their long legs and soulful eyes give them such a, oh, I dunno, maybe an arrogant look about them. You know, like they think they're the only ones that should be here and they get irritated whenever anyone else crowds them out," explained Elly as she sat, arms crossed as she leaned on the pommel of her saddle. She glanced to Reuben who sat tall in his seat, looking at his woman with a bit of an amused expression in his grin.

"What?" she asked, frowning.

"I just never thought of any animal as 'arrogant,'" answered Reuben, chuckling.

"That's cuz you only see 'em as something to shoot and eat!" she grumbled as she nudged her Appaloosa to take the lead and pushed past her man. She tried for an expression of disdain and frustration, but his broad grin brought a smile to her face, and she stifled a giggle as she shook her head.

The trail of the two outlaws, and their stolen pack

mule loaded with the goods taken from Burnett, had been easy to follow and continued on the main trail that had been used for ages if not centuries, by the many native peoples and early explorers. As they neared the summit where the mouth of the San Luis Valley opened wide its welcoming arms, the distant peaks of the Sangre de Cristos stood above the horizon of the saddle crossing. To the west and slightly behind them, another tall peak marked the end of the Sawatch Range and the beginning of the foothills of the San Juans. Nearing the edge of the trees, Elly reined up and sat looking at the vista of the valley that beckoned, glanced back to Reuben, and smiled as he came alongside.

"I will never get tired of the many beauties of God's creation!" she declared, shaking her head, and nodding toward the beginning of the granite-tipped peaks.

Reuben grinned, nodded, "Ummhmm," and stood in his stirrups to take a long gander down the valley. Nothing stirred except the tall grass waving in the breeze. On their left, the small mountain, a long black hump of timber-covered hill, was the northern anchor of the long mountain range that marched south by east into the northern reaches of the territory now known as New Mexico. This land had long been the home of the different Ute peoples with the southernmost portion populated by the Jicarilla Apache and the Navajo, while the Comanche claimed the southeastern hills and a portion of the Sangres. Now it was disputed land, with the valley a part of the proposed cede from the Tabeguache Ute as terms of the new treaty that had yet to be ratified by the U.S. Government. But the Mouache and Capote Ute were not in agreement and the many settlers and gold hunters were wanting to stake their claims.

Those disputes are what required the presence of the U.S. Marshals.

After their brief look around, they returned to the campsite used on their initial foray, choosing to use it for their nooning and to give the horses a breather and time for graze. As Reuben stepped down, Elly asked, "Could we go by the camp of the Schmidts? I've had them on my mind and I'm hopin' everything is alright with them."

"Sure, but first, while you get us some coffee goin', I'm goin' up on that little ridge yonder and have a look-see, and I'm also goin' to find the trail of those outlaws and see where they went to join the other renegades."

"You takin' Bear?"

"No, I'll leave him with you, keep you comp'ny," chuckled Reuben.

It was a bald shoulder of the ridge that Reuben chose, giving him just enough elevation to see most of the upper end of the valley and the flanks of the Sangre de Cristo Range. Belly down on a big rock, he scanned the entire area, searching for any sign of the outlaws or renegades, but also with an eye for any new settlers or sign of the Schmidt family they met on their initial journey. There was nothing amiss nor any movement until he gave a careful scan of the trees on the flanks of the northernmost Sangres. A thin wisp of smoke spiraled into the late morning sky foreshadowing more than a small cookfire, while overhead, turkey vultures glided on the mountain updraft, hanging heads searching the ground below.

With nothing stirring among the willows by the creek, no animals grazing on the tall grasses or coming to their morning water, no movement of man or beast, Reuben knew there had been some kind of commotion to cause the many animals to take shelter. With a last scan, he rose and tucked away the field glasses and took his Henry under arm to return to camp, and it was a somber-faced Reuben that walked into their small camp.

"What is it?" asked Elly, suspecting the worst.

"I think the renegades hit the Schmidt camp. Looks to be smoke comin' from there and the buzzards are circlin'."

THE STENCH OF BURNING FLESH IS UNMISTAKABLE AND unforgettable and that daunting greeting was what welcomed Reuben and Elly into the camp of the Schmidt family. A pile of charred wood and ashes still smoldered between one wheel and a hub that had fallen over the pile. Beside the ashes were the remains of Jared Schmidt, most of his body burned to ashes, but the rest were unrecognizable except for his splinted leg and part of the makeshift crutch fashioned by Reuben. Elly turned, gasped, and covered her mouth as she shook her head, anger flaring in her eyes. The mutilated body of Gertrude lay naked beside the fire ring. She had been scalped and severely abused and disfigured. Near the trees, the form of young Joel sat against the tree, blood covering his face from his scalped head. He, too, was naked, mutilated, and butchered.

Elly sat down on the log by the fire ring, elbows on her knees, as she dropped her face into her hands and began to weep. It was a quiet Reuben that stood beside her, his hand on her shoulder, offering comfort and understanding. "Why!? Why?! It's just so brutal and unnecessary!" she pleaded, knowing there was no answer that would give credence to such debauchery. She knew it was the way of fierce warriors in their belief to add more suffering to those perceived as their enemies, believing a blinded, emasculated, and dismembered enemy would wander forever in the afterlife and any bravery would revert to the warrior who did the deed.

Bear had bellied down beside Elly, laying his chin on her feet, offering the comfort of his presence. She reached down and stroked his head, "Thanks Bear, if only everybody could be like you," she consoled.

"I'm gonna get started buryin' these folks. You sit right there, and I'll get it done," offered Reuben, moving away to fetch the shovel from their pack mule.

With three graves mounded, covered with rocks, marked by charred pieces of wood from the remains of their wagon, and with a blanket of prayer, Reuben and Elly rode from the campsite, hearts filled with a blend of sadness and anger and a renewed resolve to right the wrong. Reuben led the way as they crossed the valley bottom, daring to expose themselves across the cacti and sage-covered flats. They rode side by side and Elly asked, "How far into those hills you think they've gone?"

"Dunno. The tracks I saw showed them to be walkin' their mounts, so they were in no hurry to get to the others, so I don't think they're too far into the hills. And that attack on the Schmidts happened early this morning, so they haven't gone too far either."

They had been following the obvious trail of the renegades when they left the attack on the Schmidt camp, with a band of about a dozen, there was no effort made to cover their trail and it was easy to follow. "They have no reason to believe anyone would be following so they're probably not even watching their back trail," added Reuben, "but once we get to those foothills yonder, we'll need to be almighty cautious. Instead of following direct, we'll keep to the trees and parallel their trail."

"Sounds reasonable. But if we find 'em, I want first crack at 'em!"

"So, now you've usurped God's authority and gonna take vengeance yourself?" chided Reuben.

"No, I'm just doin' it for Him!" explained Elly.

Reuben shook his head, chuckling at the reasoning of his woman and chose not to give any argument. He was also in a vengeful mood after burying the family, but he was never one to act impulsively.

10 / VENGEANCE

They traveled but an hour and chose to find a campsite. The sun was lowering in the west, and they preferred not to try tracking nor coming upon the renegades in the dark. When a likely spot showed itself, they were quick to begin the preparations for the night. After a good meal of venison steaks, yucca sprouts, cattail shoots, and onions with cornmeal biscuits, they sat back to enjoy their coffee. With the fire no more than warm coals, the smoke dissipated through the juniper, and the slight breeze wafting the odors of smoke and supper, there was nothing to give away their camp. The horses were picketed in the thicket of trees and enjoying the bunchgrass as Reuben and Elly sat contemplating the coming days.

"I know you've been thinkin' about the renegades and what you want to do, but have you thought about just how we're goin' about it?" asked Elly, slowly sipping the hot coffee as she glanced sideways at her man.

"Some, but it's kinda hard to figger, what with not knowing how many and where they are and such," answered Reuben.

"So, where does our responsibility as marshals end and our vengeance quest begin?"

"Vengeance quest? That's a little harsh, isn't it?" grumbled Reuben, frowning at Elly.

She chuckled, "And what would you call it? I know, I want to make 'em pay just as much as you do, but…" she shrugged, taking another sip of the hot java.

Reuben had finished his coffee, tossed out the dregs, and stood, his frustration showing as he walked around the camp, lifting his eyes to the palette of colors at the western horizon as the Creator showed his penchant for colorfully ending the day with splashes of pink, orange, gold and more, colors that danced across the western sky. Reuben breathed deep, taking in the wonders, and looked back at Elly who sat smiling and watching her restless man.

"I dunno. I just keep seeing the images of the bodies of that family, and each time it seems like my blood boils! I understand when natives attack settlers and such, seeking to drive them from their lands, or to get horses and goods. They're defending their homeland and trying to survive; and these are uninvited people that don't see it that way, thinking the land is empty and free for the taking. But what those renegades, and that white man who is just as bad if not worse, what they did was sheer meanness and evil!" he spat. "If all they wanted was the goods in the wagon or to drive them out of their land, they didn't have to kill 'em and mutilate them!"

"I agree, and I'm just as angry as you are, but we can't go storming into their camp and do the same thing to them!" pleaded Elly.

"We won't, and you know that. But…well, we'll just have to wait and see how it all plays out," resolved

Reuben. "For now, let's try to get us some sleep. I'm thinkin' it'll be a long day tomorrow."

First light saw the couple finishing their breakfast. Reuben had spent his time in prayer and surveying the surrounding terrain. They were about two miles into the foothills of the San Juans and in the thicker timber where the juniper and piñon were giving way to the ponderosa, spruce, and fir. As Reuben began rigging the horses, Elly finished packing the pots and plates in the parfleches. As they moved about, distant gunfire sounded to the east. Reuben looked at Elly, "That's down in the valley! Maybe some other settlers or gold hunters, but that's more shooting than a simple hunt for game," declared Reuben as the sporadic rattle of gunfire continued. He glanced to Elly, "Let's hurry and go down to see what's happening. It might be the renegades passed us by and are attacking some other camp!"

They slowed as they neared the tree line, the scattered juniper and piñon offering little cover. Although they were above the trail and the valley on the south slope of a long ridge, the cluster of juniper shielded them and they could see below where a new camp of what appeared to be gold hunters with two wagons of gear, were under attack. Reuben stepped down and went to the edge of the trees, binoculars in hand, and began scanning the attack. Elly came alongside, "What do you see?"

"Looks like the band of renegades attacking some

gold hunters. Don't appear to be any women, just a bunch of men, maybe six or eight, and they're putting up a good fight. But I think they could use some help." He handed her the binoculars and returned to the horses to retrieve his Sharps and the scope. As he walked back, he attached the scope to the rifle, checked the load, and seated himself beside the tree. Using his knees to rest his elbows, he brought up the Sharps and sighted on the attacking renegades. Taking careful aim, he steadied the rifle, took a deep breath, and let some out and slowly squeezed off his shot.

The big .52 caliber slug tore into the torso of a standing native, who had shielded himself behind a tall sage and was lifting his trade fusil for a shot at the gold hunters. The slug entered by breaking a rib under his arm, plowed through his lungs, and exited with a chunk of bone and flesh, driving the man into the prickly sage, his only sound the grunt of death. Reuben dropped the Sharps, reloading it quickly and lifted it to his shoulder for another shot. It was just shy of three hundred yards, and he slowly took aim, choosing another native for his target. Without hesitation, he squeezed off his shot, but as Reuben fired the rifle, his target dropped to one knee, causing the slug, aimed for the man's side, to blast through the top of his head, instantly killing the man.

With the staccato of intermittent rifle fire from both the renegades and the gold hunters, the renegades had not noticed the distant boom from the Sharps rifle, until Reuben took another shot and dropped another of the renegades. It was the boom that echoed across the valley that caught their attention and Elly, who had been watching through the binoculars, said, "They've heard your shots, and some are turning to look this way."

"Unless they've encountered a Sharps before, they

won't be looking this far back," surmised Reuben as he reloaded the big rifle.

"Looks like they're leaving!" stated Elly, keeping her binoculars on the attack.

Reuben looked at the scene with his scope, searching for another target, but the renegades were scurrying away, making for their horses. The couple watched as the band rallied together and turned to the west and started into the foothills, south of where Reuben and Elly were positioned. "That must be the way they came down to the valley," stated Reuben, referring to the lower trail that was beyond a pair of finger ridges that came from the foothills. He stood, returned the Sharps to the scabbard, "Let's go see that bunch down yonder, see if they need any help."

Of the six men in the group, one lay dead with a bullet wound in his head, another stood at the end of a wagon, the fletching of an arrow protruding from his thigh as he was vainly trying to remove the shaft. Four others, still in a defensive position, watched as Reuben and Elly approached. Reuben called out, "Ho! The camp! Can we come in?"

"If you're the one what was shootin' from the ridge yonder, come ahead on, and welcome!" returned the nearest man, stepping from behind the big wagon. The freighter wagons were taller, heavier, and offered more protection than the usual prairie wagon favored by settlers, and Reuben guessed one or more of these men came from a freighter company.

"I'm Reuben and this is my wife, Elly Mae. What brings you fellas up thisaway?" asked Reuben as he rode closer to the wagons, looking at the men with a seasoned eye.

"Ah, you know, lookin' for gold," answered the man. He was an average-sized man, about a half a hand under six feet, maybe weighing 160, plaid woolen britches held up by galluses, hobnail boots, and a linsey-woolsey shirt. Thick hair hung from under the short-billed cap, and muttonchop whiskers framed his ruddy face. "I'm Whitcomb! This here's Billingsley, that'ns Smart, that's his name not his intelligence, and the other'n there is Martin. The others are tendin' to their wounds.

"Say, I just wanna say thanks for doin' your shootin' while ago. We weren't doin' too good, ain't none of us marksmen, and they was gettin' almighty close. But when you opened up on 'em, musta skeered 'em sure, an' they done lit out! Didja get any?" he asked, looked to Reuben.

"Three, but since there was only 'bout a dozen of 'em, I reckon they didn't like the odds anymore. But they're likely to round up some others and be back, so stay ready, if you're of a mind on stayin' here. You do know this is Ute Indian territory, don't you?"

"Uh, no. We thought this was open country. Somebody back in Fairplay said this was good country and we might find gold down here some'eres. Since all the good claims had already been filed on, we didn't have anything to lose, so…" he shrugged.

"Yeah, the only thing you have to lose is your scalp!" declared Reuben. "But just so you'll know, this is still the land of the Ute people. Chief Ouray had agreed to cede this valley to the government as per a treaty that he signed, but the government, whoever they are, has yet to ratify that treaty and the Ute have yet to receive the promised annuities, so, it's still their land and you're trespassing."

"So, that's why the Injuns were attackin' us?" asked Whitcomb.

"No, those that were attacking you were a bunch of renegades that have nothing to do with the treaty or Chief Ouray. They were attacking you cuz they're a bunch o' murderin' thieves that like killing whites!"

"Wal, then the army should be protectin' us! Shouldn't they?" asked Whitcomb.

"I'm sure they'll get right on that, just as soon as the war is over and they get enough troops at Fort Garland, and they get trained in Indian fighting, and such. Then, maybe they'll offer a little protection to all these gold hunters and settlers that don't want to pay any attention to the treaty, that the white government is yet to sign."

Whitcomb hung his head, shaking it side to side and looked back at Reuben, "So, what're we supposed to do in the meantime? We need to find us some gold!" he groused.

"Well, I s'pose you could keep lookin' for gold, might even find some, but you won't be getting any protection from the army."

"But, what about the law? Ain't there no law here 'bouts?" asked the one known as Billingsley.

"Well, first off, what law are they supposed to enforce? You're the one's breaking the previous treaty that agreed this was the land of the Utes and you're breaking it, not them. So, should the law arrest the Indians or you?"

"Uh, I see what'chu mean. But," he paused, looking around as if he was looking for a sheriff's office or something, "is there any law around here?"

"Yup. There's two marshals that have jurisdiction

over all of the southern half of Colorado Territory. And from what I understand, they're supposed to help keep peace between the settlers and the natives, however they can."

"Where can we find 'em? You know, just in case we need 'em," asked Smart, joining the conversation.

Reuben looked around, grinned at Elly, looked back at the men, "You're lookin' at 'em."

"YOU! You're the marshal?" asked Whitcomb.

Reuben nodded, and Whitcomb continued, "But you said there were two, where's the other'n?"

Reuben grinned, nodded toward Elly, "Right there."

"Your wife!"

"Ummhmm, she's also my deputy, or I'm hers. We haven't quite got that worked out yet."

11 / SEARCH

"So, if'n we can't stay here, where we gonna go?" mumbled Whitcomb. He looked to Reuben, "If you were lookin' for gold, where would you go?"

"Look, I don't know much of anything about lookin' for gold. I do know there were some fellas that found a little color south of here on the upper reaches of the Rio Grande, but the Ute killed 'em 'fore they could get anything, so I don't think you'd wanna go there. Now, if I was to be lookin', I'd take a good look at where they've already found gold and look for country like that. You've been in South Park? Seen where they found gold?" he asked, looking from man to man as they nodded their heads.

"Now, this country doesn't look anything like that. Sure, there's mountains yonder," nodding to the Sangre de Cristos, "but nobody's found any gold there. So, I'd be for lookin' up north, maybe west of South Park cuz just over those mountains on the west side, they found gold in an area called California Gulch, it's near the headwaters of the Arkansas River. But, from what I hear, nobody's gone further west into those mountains. That's where I'd be lookin' if I was lookin' for gold."

The men looked at one another, nodding and agreeing, and Whitcomb looked back to Reuben. "And that land is not Injun country?"

"Well, I can't guarantee you won't run into some natives up thataway, but that area *is* open for settlement and gold hunting."

"So, how do we get there?" asked Billingsley.

Reuben nodded to the north end of the valley, "There's a pass yonder, and a good trail that'll take you down to the Arkansas Valley. Follow the river north till you find yourself a good spot and file a claim and start diggin'!"

REUBEN AND ELLY SAT ON THEIR MOUNTS, WATCHING THE two wagons, each pulled by four mules, and the gold hunters as they started to the north end of the valley. They left a grave behind them, and one man turned to wave and Reuben lifted his hand in return. Elly asked, "Think they'll find gold?"

"Hard to say. They didn't impress me as knowing very much or having any experience at hunting gold. They'd prob'ly make more money haulin' supplies in those wagons to the other miners."

"So, what're *we* doing now?" asked Elly, turning her attention away from the departing group.

Reuben leaned his left elbow on the pommel as he twisted around to look at his woman, "When you were watching the attack, did you see that big whisker-faced white man?"

Elly frowned, "No, I didn't." She faced Reuben, "Are you thinking that was a different band of natives?"

"I dunno. But if it is, there's more trouble here than we bargained for, but I think I'd like to make sure. My concern is for the bunch with the white men. If it was just a war party of Utes, then that's the army's problem, but with the white men, then it's our problem."

"How we gonna find out?"

Reuben sat up, lifted his eyes to the sun and calculated there to be about a half day of light left. "I think we need to find out, but I'm not anxious to be caught by them. There should be a big moon tonight, I think it's comin' on to a full moon, and maybe if we travel at night, it'd be safer. With so many in their war party, their tracks should be easy to follow."

With a nod toward the dead bodies of the raiders, Elly asked, "What about them?"

"Yeah. Usually, they come back for their dead, and I don't want to be here when they do." He stood in his stirrups to look up the draw where the war party fled, "Maybe we can take to the trees yonder, don't make a fire till later, and keep a watch to see if they return. Either way, we can still follow the tracks to their camp."

Just south of them stood a handful of timbered hills, the most prominent appearing to be a collapsed volcanic cone, dark basaltic rock littering the north slope. It stood apart from the other foothills of the San Juans and showed as a landmark to the long valley of the Kerber Creek, one of the few creeks that carried live water into the basin of the valley. It was that valley that held the tracks of the fleeing war party. Reuben pointed, "Let's head thataway, maybe we can find some live water and a place to make camp away from the trail."

"Sounds good to me. I could use an afternoon of rest, maybe a good nap in the shade," she chuckled as she looked at her man.

Although the mouth of the valley or gulch was wide, it quickly narrowed to about a quarter mile and just into the gulch, they spotted a trickle of water coming from a break in the hills to their right, north of the valley. Reuben nodded as Elly pointed and led the way into the smaller arroyo to search out a camp with good tree cover. Knowing Reuben's habit for wanting a high point to scan the territory, she knew he would not lack for choices as they pushed into the narrow defile.

"Let's just do a cold camp," declared Reuben, "Don't wanna give ourselves away to the Utes and if we're goin' to make our move after sundown, we'll do alright with pemmican and such."

"Suits me. All I want right now is a good nap. If we're travelin' after dark, it might do you good, too."

"I wanna have a good look-see, maybe watch to see if they come after the bodies of the downed warriors. That'd make trailin' 'em easier."

"Then you take care of the horses and I'll roll out our bedrolls in the shade, get us some pemmican and the leftover biscuits from this mornin'," offered a smiling Elly as she watched Reuben step down and take the reins of both horses and the lead to the pack mule. Elly lay out the bedrolls and went to the packs, now stacked under the long swooping branches of a big spruce, to get their meal makings. She thought about Reuben's habit of having his coffee but shook her head and determined to make a cold camp without any coffee.

"I'm headed up that rise yonder," stated Reuben, nodding to the slope on the far side of the little creek below their camp. "Bear'll stay here with you and I might be a while, wanna give the renegades time to come back for their dead."

"Looks like that'll be a good walk, you takin' the Sharps?" asked a concerned Elly, for he would be about a mile from their camp.

"Yeah, but that's the only point where I can see back to the site of the attack as well as the valley below us where they went when they left the fight." He paused as he watched Elly crawl onto the blankets in the shade of the tall tree, noting she had laid the Henry beside her. "Back soon!" he added as he turned away and started to the creek just below their camp. He stretched his long legs and hopped across the shallow stream with one step on a rock in the middle and the other to the bank. He strode up the timbered slope and within moments crested the small knoll. With scattered juniper and piñon, interspersed with limestone and sandstone slabs, he easily found his promontory and stretched out for a good view of the wide San Luis Valley to the north and south, and the small valley that bore to the west and carried the small Kerber Creek into the open expanse of the bigger valley.

With binoculars in hand, he made his usual scan of the territory before him, then focused in on the site of the morning's attack on the freight wagons and the gold hunters. Although the sage and greasewood hampered his view of the bodies, he remembered about where they lay and from his point of view, could see nothing that told of any visitors to the area. Satisfied, he started his thorough search back from the attack site to the valley behind where the Ute war party had fled. He had twisted around and lay with one elbow on the ground when he spotted riders coming on the trail beside the willow-lined creek. Ute! He lowered the binoculars, checked the position of the sun, and doffed his hat to use the brim to shade the lenses of the field glasses, concerned about any reflection of the lowering sun that might give away his position.

With the clumsy hold on the binoculars, holding the hat with brim extended over the end, he watched the war party come from the valley. He was surprised to see more than had been in the original attacking group, he counted over twenty warriors. He scanned them as best he could, searching for the white men, but there were none. He dropped his glasses, watched the band move closer, leave the trail, and take to the shoulders of the foothills to round the point and turn toward the attack site.

It was just a short while later that the band returned with the bodies of the downed attackers, but rather than returning to the trail up Kerber Creek, they continued due south, staying east of the collapsed volcanic dome, and rounded the wide point of foothills and disappeared to the west beyond the range of hills that stretched east to west toward the greater San Juans. Reuben frowned, wondering what they were doing. *Now, that's strange. Usually when they fetch the bodies of their downed brothers, they return to the village for the families to tend to the bodies and bury them, or whatever they do. Hmm, maybe their village is beyond that ridge, not up this draw.*

He took another broad scan of the valley before him, searching for any other sign of settlers or natives, but seeing nothing but a scampering and frolicking herd of antelope, fawns playfully enjoying the day, he rose from his promontory and started back to camp. When he walked into the camp, Bear opened one eye but refused to lift his head off his paws, closed it and returned to his snooze. Elly did not stir. He went to the packs, fetched the coffeepot and the bag of coffee, and started to the creek for some fresh water, determined to have his coffee.

12 / OUTLAWS

The big man looked like the little brother of a grizzly bear, whiskery face, long scraggly hair, deep chested and looking more like a whiskey barrel than a man, he stood with a M61 Springfield musket cradled in his arms folded across his chest. He had a Spencer carbine but had been unable to get cartridges for the weapon and was satisfied with his dependable Springfield. Although called Bear Face by the Ute leader, his name was Horace Hickam when he and his companions had been in the 5th Texas Mounted Rifles, a Confederate company in the battle of Glorieta Pass in the early days of the war. But at their first opportunity, the three men had deserted, taking their weapons and horses with them. When the Confederates were forced to retreat to Santa Fe because of lack of supplies, Hickam and company made their escape.

Hickam watched as Louis Franklin, *Freckles,* and Ed Przyzycki, *Pork,* rode slowly up the draw that was thick with aspen and cottonwood that sided the little Clover Creek. Hickam pulled a plug of tobacco from his pocket and bit off a chew that prompted exaggerated chewing until he was able to maneuver the plug into the side of his mouth. He spat into the brush at his side, and hailed the two men, motioning them into the campsite just back from the creek in a little hollow of a draw holding a dry bed runoff creek.

As they neared, he growled, "Where ya been?"

"Got held up in the village," began Freckles as he swung down from his mount.

"I see ya got yerself a new horse," growled Hickam, walking closer and looking at the packhorse and the packs. "Get what we need?"

"Mostly, and some other stuff. We was in a hurry and got what we could."

Hickam frowned, glaring at the two men, waiting for an explanation. His lip curled in a snarl, "Well?"

"We hit the couple with two wagons, they was in their cabin, and had 'em covered and I had the man at his wagon, showin' what he had, then a pair o' marshals caught us from behind!"

Hickam turned, "Marshals?"

Freckles nodded his head, glanced at Pork, and said, "Ummhmm. Hadn't seen 'em 'fore, an' they came up behin' us. Took our weapons, tied us up an' locked us in a shed." He chuckled, letting a grin split his face, "But we cut ourselves loose, broke outta the cabin, stole the horses and practically emptied his wagon!" he cackled at the memory.

"Din't they follow you?"

"Never seen 'em. We got away late in the night, an' had more'n half a day head start. Don't think any them settlers were of a mind to foller us, an' mebbe them marshals was gone," he shrugged.

"You leave a trail they can foller?" asked Hickam.

Freckles glanced at Pork, shrugged and answered, "Nah, we was careful. Kept to the rocks an' such."

Hickam looked skeptically at both men, shook his head, and growled, "Get them packs off, let me see what'chu got."

THE COFFEEPOT DANCED ON THE ROCK AS THE SMELL OF coffee filled the little campsite, bringing Elly awake and frowning. She looked at Reuben, sat up, and asked, "I thought we were having a cold camp?"

"You know me—gotta have my coffee!" he grinned as he poured two cups and offered one to a sleepy-eyed Elly. "But I don't think we need be concerned; I watched what I think was a different village of Utes come from the valley yonder, looked to be a bigger band than we expected, but they turned south and disappeared around the point," nodding to the hills and ridges to the south. "They're the ones that attacked the freight wagons alright, but after gettin' their dead, they kept goin' south. No white men among 'em."

Elly frowned, sipped the hot coffee, and looked up at Reuben, "So, whadda we do now?"

"I think we need to go back to the trail left by the two outlaws we were chasin' 'fore the attack on the wagons. Maybe we can do as we first thought, follow their trail to the camp of the band of renegades and their partner, the big one with the whiskers."

"Well, chasin' outlaw white men is a little more in line with our duties," resolved Elly.

She frowned as she thought about it, "We were goin' to travel after dark, that still the plan?"

"We could, should be easy to find where we left off

the trail. Or we could just get an early start in the mornin', maybe 'fore first light. That way, we could stay on the trail till we get to their camp. Might be a little safer in the daylight."

Elly shook her head, finished the coffee, and tossed out the dregs. After setting the cup down beside her bedroll, she rubbed the scruff on Bear's neck, lay back, pulled up the covers and rolled over to her side, facing away from Reuben. "Wake me when you're ready to leave," she muttered.

"Hey! What about supper?"

"Cold camp, remember?" she replied, stifling a snicker.

THE LANTERNS OF THE NIGHT HAD SNUFFED OUT THEIR flames as the thin grey line of early morning made the Sangre de Cristo Mountains nothing more than a jagged silhouette of darkness. To the west, darkness still shadowed the distant San Juan Mountains, and the last of the stars began to blink their final flicker of light. Reuben and Elly kept to the flanks of the foothills, making their own trail below the tree line, as they pushed north on the west edge of the San Luis Valley. As the finger ridges from the foothills stretched into the valley floor, seeking out the ridges from the eastern mountains, the valley narrowed. Their goal was the north end of the valley where the two men that had stolen the goods from the trader at the foot of Poncha Pass, had turned into the foothills. Believing them to be bound for a meeting with the renegade with the Utes and White Skunk, Reuben and Elly wanted to find their camp before deciding a course of action.

They had gone but a few miles when an ancient trail dropped from the trees and pointed north. Although the main trail and rough wagon road in the valley was pioneered by Bautista de Anza in 1779, its continued use by soldiers from Fort Garland, trappers searching for prime streams, and other pioneers, had made it the best trail but it lay in the open below the ridges and tree line. The trail they now followed, showed sign of being both a game trail and a trail of the ancients that moved through this land in eons past. When they passed an old cairn of stones, Reuben's mind traveled into history wondering who and when the cairn told of their passing.

They were approaching one of the few live streams that came from the western mountains when Bear stopped, head lifted, one paw held out as he emitted a low growl of warning. "What is it, boy?" asked Elly as she reined her Appaloosa beside the big dog.

She looked toward the willows and cottonwoods that lined the creek about a hundred yards ahead but saw nothing. She glanced back to Reuben, turned to look again at the stream, frowned and stood in her stirrups as she shaded her eyes to the long lances of gold that bent over the eastern mountains to light the valley bottom. She dropped into the seat of her saddle as she twisted to face Reuben, "Bears, black bear!" she pointed toward the willows.

Reuben moved beside her, looked at the green willows and more that told of the creek and saw what looked like a black bear face-off. As they watched, they saw a pair of cubs behind the black bear on the uphill side of the creek, while below another bear, cinnamon in color, rose to his hind legs, pawing at the air as he let out a scratchy growl.

"Looks like a boar is goin' after the cubs and that mama bear ain't about to let him!" declared Elly.

"Yeah, but that boar looks a bit bigger," replied Reuben.

"No matter, she'll whip him. That's what a mama does!"

The boar dropped to all fours and started for the sow, growling and snapping as he started his charge. As he neared the sow, he humped his back and lay back his ears, bared his teeth and bit at her neck. But the sow tore into him, slapping at his face with long claws, biting at his neck, growling, and snapping. The boar backed up, and dove in again for another attack, but the sow dodged his attack and slapped at his head as he passed, drawing blood on the top of his head. He shook his head at the irritation, dug at it with his paw, and sat back, looking and growling at the sow, but the sow turned, scampered to her cubs and with a barked command the family of three crashed through the willows, splashed through the creek, and left the cinnamon boar to watch, probably counting himself lucky she did not continue the fight. The boar relaxed, shook his head side to side, and ambled upstream along the willows and disappeared into the thickets of cottonwoods and aspen.

Elly grinned, looked at Reuben, "Told ya! Ya don't mess with a mama protecting her young! Ain't safe!"

Reuben grinned, shaking his head, "I think it's safer to go after those outlaws and renegades!" He nudged Blue and took the lead as they pushed through the willows, crossing the little stream, and riding on north.

13 / TRACKS

Less than two miles further on, Reuben frowned, reining up and motioning for Elly to come alongside. He nodded to the thicket of aspen and cottonwood that shrouded the creek below and pointed to the bald hillside beyond. "That's high ground, and there's prob'ly timber on the other side. Although that," nodding to the thicket, "looks a little more invitin', we're too close to where the renegades were to get comfortable. Let's move over that ridge yonder, and if there's cover and water, we'll noon there."

Elly frowned, looking at her man, and asked, "You have a feeling about something wrong?"

"Maybe, not sure, but let's not take any chances."

She nodded and nudged the Appy to take the lead, motioning Bear to scout, and with Reuben bringing up the rear as he led the pack mule, she started toward the lower end of the thicket to cross the creek. Just before the creek, they crossed a well-used trail that sided the creek and disappeared into the trees. Elly pointed to it as she passed but kept moving. It was no more than five hundred yards to the crest of the ridge and Bear stopped, looking back to the west toward the creek and turning back to look just before him. Elly saw what she thought was a game trail and moved closer, leaning down for a closer look, and quickly sat upright, twisting around to face Reuben. "Take a gander at those tracks! I think they're the outlaws we were following!"

Reuben stepped down and went to one knee beside the trail, reaching out to touch the edges of the tracks. He looked at each one, nodded, and stood to look in the direction of the tracks. "Looks like they went toward those aspen, but I think the trail rides this bald slope but disappears into the trees yonder. What with that first trail we crossed, and now this one, I'm sure these," pointing to the tracks at his feet, "were the outlaws." He shaded his eyes, looked down at the tracks again, and turned to look at the low ridge that rose to the peak of a timber-covered mountain. To the right or north, the ridge dropped into a shallow draw that came from the peak and emptied into the big valley.

"Those tracks *are* those of the outlaws. I remember the tracks of those mules, and they're headin' to their rendezvous with their boss man and the renegades." He looked again at the shallow draw, nodded toward it, "You find us a spot for noonin' down yonder, lead the horses and I'll follow on foot. I want to try to cover our tracks a mite, don't want to give ourselves away to them."

Elly nodded and accepted the offered reins and lead line of the roan and the mule, then started to the trees at the bottom of the long ridge. Reuben watched her for a moment before going to the scattered juniper and cutting a branch from the backside and returning to the tracks. He knew he could not just wipe them out with the branch because the marks of the branch are just as obvious as the tracks, but using the branch, dragging it behind him, he walked back down the slope toward the creek, stepping on the tracks they made just moments before. On his return, he was careful where he stepped and continually scattered dirt, grasses, rocks, and bits of cactus. He knew it would not fool an experienced tracker that was on their trail, but it might slow down the casual follower or even obscure the sign enough to prevent a passerby more intent on his own movements than any other. He went to the trees and worked his way down the north side of the ridge toward where he expected to find Elly and the horses.

"It won't totally fool anyone, but lookin' at those clouds, I'm thinkin' we might get some rain, at least some wind, and that'll help more'n anything," he said as he walked toward Elly. She had loosened the girths on the horses and mule and was digging through a parfleche for some pemmican and more. She looked up, smiled, "And hopefully, we'll be long gone 'fore anyone comes lookin'!"

It was just past midday when they started up the long gulley. "This gulley parallels the creek in the bottom yonder, where the renegades took that trail. I figger we can stay outta sight and safer by followin' 'em from this side of the ridge. We'll check things out now and again," explained Reuben as he sat twisted around on his seat, one hand on the cantle as he spoke to Elly following close behind.

"I thought as much," answered a smiling Elly, knowing her man and his cautious ways, especially when she was with him.

It was a steady but easy climb, with the only hindrance being a stretch of blowdown where at some time the high winds of the mountains wrought havoc on the thick growing pines in the bottom of the gulley, laying them down as if the new growth had been humbled before the forces of nature. But a narrow game trail kept to the edge of the trees and wound its way always upward. In about a mile and a half, they came to the first saddle notch where the timber thinned and Reuben reined up, motioning for Elly to stay back. With binoculars and Henry rifle in hand, he swung down and, in a crouch, moved to the crest of the ridge on his left.

He bellied down and crawled under a long juniper branch and lifted his binoculars to search the hillsides and valley bottom below. This was the valley with the trail taken by the outlaws and Reuben quickly spotted the trail and followed it as far as he could with his field glasses. There was no movement, but it was evident by the churned soil, the trail below had seen many horses.

After a thorough scan of the valley below, he crabbed back from the tree, stood, and looked around at the hill-tops and the peaks beyond. The nearest bald peak had a lesser shoulder, with the tall peak that appeared to be squared off but dropping steeply away. Further beyond several taller peaks stood, their bald heads lifting rugged shoulders high above the timberline. Reuben looked over the saddle notch to the valley below, and back to the timbered hills and ridges beyond. He noted the long line of hills paralleled the 'S' curves of the valley with the little creek and knew any long encampment by the rene-gades would be near water. He turned back to Elly, "We'll stay in the trees, move slow and as quiet as possi-ble, and before crossing any ridge or such like, we'll need to reconnoiter."

Elly nodded, understanding, and trusting her man. Reuben swung back aboard his roan and started off, wending through the thick forest of spruce, fir, and pines. As he neared the crest of another long saddle, he held up his hand, motioned for Bear to come back close, and stepped down. Cresting the ridge, he looked down into a little swale with a small pond, several aspen, and good thick cover. He nodded to himself, looked at the thick timbered hillside above the arroyo and the hills beyond, nodded again, and turned back to return to Elly's side. "There's a bit of a pond down below, looks clear so it must be spring fed. Might make a good camp for us, depending on where the others are, but I think we'll stop there, and I'll scout a little further on foot." He looked to the darkening sky and the rolling dark clouds, "I think we're gonna be in for a bit of a storm so we might need to make us some shelter, too."

"As long as there are plenty of trees, shouldn't be too hard," answered Elly, "but lookin' at those clouds, we don't have much time."

Reuben nodded and returned to Blue, mounted up and started through the trees on a trail previously chosen, that would take them to the arroyo bottom. A quick glance to the sky showed the clouds were pulling the plug on the rain as big drops began to splash through the trees. The usual whisper of wind through the pines turned into a low howl as the tall trees bent and swayed to the stormy gusts. As they entered the little clearing on the uphill bank of the pond, Reuben swung down, caught the reins of Blue and Elly's Appy, grabbed the lead of the mule, and led the animals into the tall spruce, tethering them on long leads until they could get some cover erected. Elly had grabbed some rope and rawhide thongs from the panniers, and with her hatchet in hand, began cutting branches for the cover of a lean-to. Reuben quickly cut a long sapling, stripped it, and lay it between two strong branches of spruce that stood near one another. The practiced pair soon had the makings of a lean-to, layering branches across the crossties and to the ground, tying them secure, stretching one of the ground covers over the top and one on the ground underneath. Within a short while, they had a secure lean-to, bedrolls underneath, a space for saddles and other gear under cover of a tall spruce with long branches. Satisfied with their cover, Reuben returned to the animals and finished stripping the rest of the gear and picketing them on leads that stretched to good cover.

When he returned to the camp, Elly had rolled out the blankets, had a pouch of pemmican and a canteen of water between, and sat smiling at her man as he ducked under the lean-to, grinning at his woman. "Well, guess I won't go on that scout after all!"

"Wouldn't do no good," agreed Elly. "Maybe we can get some rest while this storm gives us good cover."

"Hope so, but as soon as it lets up, I need to scout around. I think we might be pretty close to 'em and wouldn't want to give ourselves away by lettin' 'em smell smoke or somethin' like that." He was stretched out, legs crossed at his ankles and leaning on one elbow as he munched on the pemmican. He frowned, thinking, glanced at Elly, and said, "Look, if somethin' was to happen to me, you light out for the fort and get to safety with the soldiers."

Elly frowned at him, "How come you to say that? You've never been concerned about things like that before."

"I dunno, maybe it's cuz these are all renegades and outlaws, and none of 'em are any good. And the way that one looked at you and the trader's wife, I just don't like it!" He paused a moment, thoughtful, "Say, didn't that lieutenant back to the fort say somethin' 'bout makin' a patrol or somethin'?"

"Yes, he did. When we left, the lieutenant was leaving later that same day. He was making a patrol to the west, then going north and around the upper end and back down the east side to the fort."

"Then, they oughta be comin' thisaway purty soon, huh?"

Elly shrugged, pursed her lips as she raised one eyebrow, "Yeah, why?"

"Cuz if we need help, they should be easy to find and not too far away. So, if you can find 'em, that'd be a help."

"If *I* can find 'em?"

"Yeah, you know, if somethin' happens and you need some help."

"Now, you know I can take care of myself!"

"Yeah, and so can I, but there's a few more of 'em than just us two," answered Reuben.

Elly turned to look at Reuben, frowning, "You're really afraid of this, aren't you?"

He shook his head, "I...well, I just...I dunno, it's just one o' those feelin's, you know?"

"Then maybe we oughta just head on out of here right now, if that's the way you feel."

"Not in this storm!" he declared, looking at the downpour that seemed to be increasing. It had started as a blowing cloudburst, but was settling into a steady deluge, with the wind continuing to howl and toss the trees about. He looked back at his woman, forced a grin, "Ah, it's prob'ly nothin'. We'll just wait out this storm and then..." he shrugged.

14 / DISCOVERY

The dim light of early morning showed clouds and fog lay low in the draws and valleys while timbered hilltops and mountain crags stood tall as ghosts coming from the mist. Proud shoulders lifting arrogant granite tips to snatch at thin lances of light stretching high into the grey sky and cast wispy shadows across the wilderness. Reuben sat on the flat limestone rock that teetered atop a smaller fulcrum, his feet on solid ground, and looked about across the eerie scene. He was certain they were near the encampment of the renegade band of Utes that had been joined by the outlaw gold hunters, but he was in no hurry to confront the bunch. Since yesterday afternoon when the storm blew up, he had a premonition of peril and danger. He shook his head as he lifted his eyes heavenward and began to pray.

As he prayed, the words of Psalm 23 echoed in his mind, *Yea, though I walk through the valley of the shadow of death, I will fear no evil, for thou art with me.* He did not ask for deliverance, but for the presence of God as he sought to do his duty and confront the evil, perhaps bring them to justice or even deliver that justice. He rose, giving one last glance to the valley below, and started back to the camp. Elly was waiting, a hat-sized fire with the coffeepot dancing and the thin spiral of smoke dissipating in the branches and needles of the tall ponderosa. She smiled as he came into the camp, the dim light of early morning shadows and the heavy clouds masking their presence, as she held out the cup of steaming coffee as he neared.

With a glance to the eastern sky, Reuben sipped on the coffee, sat the cup down on the rock, "I'll saddle the horses and mule, leave the girths loose, just in case we need to make a quick getaway," he said with a droll, a smile splitting his face. He quickly rigged the animals and with his Henry under arm, he gave Elly a warm embrace, nodded, and stepped into the woods. Elly lifted her eyes to Heaven and muttered a quick prayer and returned to the fire to pour herself a cup of coffee.

Everything was wet. But the wet needles beneath the many pines masked Reuben's movements through the woods. He moved uphill and west, working toward the top of the forested hill that stood between his camp and where he believed the renegades had made their encampment. As he neared the crest, he slowed, ever watchful, the sky slowly fading from grey to pale blue off his left shoulder. He slipped his binoculars from the case at his side and bellied down beneath a big fir, he scanned the small parklike clearings in the basin below. As he searched the trees, he scanned four clearings that lay below. The larger one to the right, about a hundred yards by thirty, held the horses, about twenty head. As he continued his scan, he spotted several hastily fashioned shelters under the bigger trees of the center clearing that was about two hundred feet wide and long, while in the lower clearing, three horses and two mules were tethered in the trees and some canvas shelters stood below the long branches of a tall spruce. *That's gotta be the white men, one of 'em rode a mule, and they stole one from the trader.*

He wanted to be closer, needful of knowing these were the Utes that had attacked the Schmidt camp and killed the family. The only way he could know for sure, was to see if any of those horses were from the Schmidts or if there was any other plunder that told for certain these had killed their friends. With a quick glance around, looking to the east and the beginning of the day with the sky showing blue, and the foggy clouds in the vales slowly fading. He replaced the binoculars in the case, moved back from the crest and started through the trees, moving toward the upper clearing with the horses.

The clearing reminded him of a long ladle, the upper end to his right swooping up toward the ridge that came from the higher hilltop beyond on the south side. He came as a ghost, his steps silenced by the damp aspen leaves and pine needles that covered the floor of the woods. He stepped beside the rough-barked ponderosa as he searched the clearing, looking at each of the horses. He remembered the Schmidts having a matched pair of black Percheron cross dray horses and a bay and a sorrel riding horses. He frowned, shading his eyes as he focused on the herd. The animals had gathered on the far side of the clearing where a bit of a stream, probably a spring, had made the grass green and offered better graze. He thought he recognized the team but wanted to be certain. He glanced around, picked up a palm-sized stone and threw it at the herd, startling the animals, making them move around. As the nearest horses moved away, he saw the team and nodded to himself, knowing those were the horses from the Schmidts, confirming this band was the one that attacked the camp of his friends.

He started to turn, but was struck from behind, making his knees buckle and his head drop forward as pain and blackness enveloped him. As he cratered to the ground, he had a passing image of Elly, alone in the camp. The same wetness that cloaked Reuben's approach to the horses, also silenced the approach of the sole guard that had been left to watch the horses. He thought he saw movement, worked his way through the trees, uncertain of what was there. But when the stone was thrown and the man moved, the warrior Pichiute, lifted his war club and dropped the white man to the ground. He shouted his war cry, slipped his rifle that was slung on his back and fired a round into the air to alert the camp.

The shot brought all the warriors and the white men from their blankets, some still staggering in sleep, rubbing their eyes, others with weapons in hand searching the trees for attackers. The shouted cry from the next clearing with the horses prompted White Skunk to motion to three warriors to go to the clearing. The others were waved into the trees, taking a defensive position. As the others scattered, the white man called Bear Face pushed through the trees and oak brush, rifle in hand, looking for any attackers. White Skunk nodded, *"Kwiyagat(ü) kova!* Bear Face, no one attacks, my warrior with the horses shouted for help." He turned toward the upper park, saw his men returning, a man hanging between them. He frowned and stepped toward the men, looking at the man. He grabbed his hair and lifted his head, "Aiieee! This is the one with the far-shooting rifle! He was with those at the wagon and shot your hat!"

Bear Face came closer, looked at the man and snarled, "You gonna kill 'im?"

As they talked, Freckles and Pork had followed Hickam from the trees and looked at the man. Freckles said, "Hey! He's that marshal we tol' you 'bout!" pointing at the sagging form of Reuben.

"He's the marshal?" asked Hickam, looking from Reuben to Freckles, glancing at White Skunk and back to Reuben.

"Ummhmm," answered Freckles, craning to look past the warriors holding Reuben, "Where's his deputy? That woman?"

Skunk scowled at the white men, looked at his warriors, "Is there another? A woman?" he asked, remembering the woman that had stood with the man at the camp of the wagon. She had held a rifle on him, keeping him from striking this man now hanging between his men.

Pichiute looked at their leader, "No, he is alone!"

Skunk looked at his men, back at the white men, and growled, "You!" pointing to Pichiute, "take one man, backtrack this one, find the woman and bring her here!"

Pichiute slapped one of the men on the arm holding Reuben, nodded, and the two men went to their blankets, grabbing their other weapons and soon disappeared into the trees, returning to where they had taken the white man, and started on his back trail. Although the wet leaves and needles quieted the movements of someone passing, the tracks could easily be followed, each footprint showing clearly on the wet floor.

Elly had just tossed out the dregs of her coffee when Bear came to his feet, looking into the trees. The distant sound of a gunshot racketed through the hills, and Elly froze, looking at Bear and into the trees, trying to will Reuben's appearance. But nothing stirred, no other sound came, and Elly's spine tingled as she searched the trees and listened. She moved to the side of Bear, dropped to one knee beside him and put her arm over his shoulders, "What is it, boy? What do you hear?"

Bear did not move, did not respond, yet stared into the trees. A low growl rumbled in his chest, and he turned to look at Elly, back to the trees. "Is it Reuben, boy?" but she knew Bear would not be growling at the return of her man, only danger prompted this reaction. She wanted to give Reuben ample time to return, but if there was a problem, should she go for help, or try to do it herself? She shook her head and started to the horses. She went to the Appy, tightened the girth, and started to Blue, when Bear, now beside her, growled. Elly dropped her hand to the Colt at her hip and slipped it from the holster, cocking the hammer as she moved.

Two warriors stepped from the trees, one with a rifle held at his side, pointing it at her as he snarled, "You, *wüüram!* Come with! Now!" Bear had slipped under the belly of Blue and moved into the trees, and Elly knew he was moving behind the warriors. She was between the horses, looking over the back of her horse, "I will not go with you!" she growled. "Where is my man?" As she spoke, she slowly lifted her pistol, looking from the man with the rifle who had spoken, to the one with a bow and nocked arrow that stood at his side, scowling at her.

Bear came from behind the men, slightly to the side of the one with the rifle, and launched himself at the man, teeth bared, eyes flaring, and paws outstretched.

The big black dog, larger than most wolves, struck fear into the warriors, but the first warrior had no time to move, and the fangs of Bear sunk into his neck, the weight of the dog and the force of his rush, driving him to the ground. The second warrior, also startled, stepped sideways, but the force of the charge drove Pichiute into him, knocking him to the side. As he struggled for his footing, the pistol of the woman blasted, and the bullet tore into the man's throat. Although Elly had aimed for the man's chest, the collision with the first warrior made the bullet plow through the man's neck, blasting out the side of his head and dropping him to the ground.

Bear had driven Pichiute to the ground, and his teeth tore the man's throat away. The warrior tried to fight, but the ripping and tearing at his throat and neck, also ripped his life from his body and Elly called Bear, "Bear! Here boy!" slapping her hand to the saddle. As Bear lifted his head, blood dripping from his jowls, he looked at Elly. She searched the trees for other warriors, bringing the Colt to full cock as she looked. Bear came to her side, and she dropped her hand to his scruff, still looking. She lowered the hammer, slipped the pistol into the holster, and quickly tightened the girth on Blue and the pack mule. She swung aboard, and slapped legs to the Appaloosa and with a glance over her shoulder, leads in hand, took to the trail to the bottom of the arroyo that carried Clover Creek into the big San Luis Valley. She was determined to find the patrol of soldiers, and bring them back to get her man, nothing less would do, he must be saved!

15 / VILLAGE

The throbbing in his head brought him slowly to consciousness. He started to reach to his head to feel for a wound, but his hands would not move. He frowned, slowly opening his eyes just a slit to look around as he struggled with his hands behind his back. He realized he was bound, his head hurt with an excruciating pain, and he stifled a moan. He tried not to move, peering through the slit of his eyelids to look around, and saw several warriors, seated and standing about, talking, and gesturing toward him and looking at others. A big man, probably the leader, stood with his back to Reuben talking with another man that he could not see, but growled as he spoke. The other man stepped to the side to look at Reuben and was instantly recognized as the white man with the black whiskery face he had heard called Bear Face.

"Whatchu mean you wanna take him to the village?!" growled Bear, looking back at the leader, White Skunk.

"When we take captives and horses and more to the village, other warriors will see and want to join us! We need more warriors and Chief Cuchutikay does not want them to go to fight the white men with us! But with this," he motioned to the stack of stolen goods including the rifles taken from the Schmidts, "and the horses and that," snarling toward the captive Reuben, "other warriors will want to join us!"

"You don't need that to get more warriors! All you need is to take me to that gold," growled Hickam, nodding to the gold nugget that hung at White Skunk's chest, "an' you can buy all the rifles and ammunition you need to outfit your men and more b'sides! If them others know they can get good rifles, they'll come with you no matter what that chief says!"

"I do not know if there is more gold! This one," grabbing at the big nugget, "was in the water and I did not see any more!"

Bear Face, or Hickam, shook his head, growling, "Look Skunk, you tell me where you got it and me'n my men will go see if there's more. You can go to your village, get your warriors, and I'll get the gold and go to the traders and buy you some rifles and ammunition! We'll meet back here in a couple days, and I'll have the rifles for your men and then you can make war against all them white settlers you want!" His growl had turned into more of a whine as he spoke, pleading with the war leader of the Ute.

White Skunk glared at the bushy-faced white man, thinking as he looked. He had thought about getting rid of this man and his two followers but believed he could be used to get goods from the white traders. Now as he thought about the possibility of more rifles, he considered doing as the man said, knowing he could always find them later and take their weapons off their dead bodies. He stepped closer to Bear Face. "Where is trader with rifles?"

Hickam unconsciously stepped back slightly, "Why, just down the pass yonder, in that settlement in the big valley with the river. My men got some supplies there just th' other day! He's got lots of rifles and such for trade there. And with a little bit o' gold, we can pro'ly get enough for all your men!"

White Skunk glared at the man, cocking one eyebrow up as he stared, then dropped to one knee, picked up a stick and began drawing in the dirt. He jabbed the stick into the dirt, looked at Hickam, "Here," he pointed to the rise behind Hickam, "over ridge, below is creek." He drew in the dirt a squiggly line for the creek, showed it joining another and looked up, pointed over Hickam's shoulder, "Mountain there," and jabbed the dirt map again, showed the second creek splitting to both sides of the mountain, and pointed to the north fork of the creek, "Here!" He stood, turning away, and Hickam looked again at the map, turned to look at the distant peak that rose behind another nearer peak, and began to let a grin split his face. Rotten tobacco-stained teeth showed from behind the whiskers as he turned to Freckles. "You two, get them horses and that mule ready! We're goin' after gold!"

Hickam looked at the captive white man who was tied with hands behind his back and tied to a tree. Hickam chuckled, cackled as he walked to the man, "Wal, Marshal, we're gonna be leavin' you now. Prob'ly won't be seein' you again, seein' as how ol' Skunk there tol' us where to find the gold. 'Sides, he's takin' you to his village, gonna use you to try to get him some more warriors, then they'll prob'ly torture you to death, see if they can make you scream. Wish I could be there to see that, but I'm thinkin' there's some nuggets that are callin' my name! Hehehehe!" cackled the big man as he reached out and slapped Reuben, backhanding him and kicking his knee, trying to cripple him.

"Just in case he lets you loose, that oughta keep you from follerin' us! Cuz we'll be watchin' fer ya, and we can do more'n any Injun can do!" he laughed as he turned away to join his two companions.

The white men were riding from the camp when White Skunk began ordering his men about. In moments, the horses had been brought into camp and Reuben lifted atop the sorrel that had belonged to Jared Schmidt. The warriors tied his feet together with a long thong under the belly of the horse, his hands still tied behind his back, and the lead line handed to a mounted warrior that waited beside White Skunk. The war leader looked at Reuben and growled. "My warriors went after your woman. They will bring her to the village after they are finished with her, if she still lives!" He snarled at Reuben, with the corner of his lip lifting as he glared at his captive. "They will have your woman, your horses, and your far-shooting rifle that will be mine!"

Reuben did not respond, refusing to give the war leader any satisfaction with his response. He did his best to look bored and disinterested, but he feared for Elly and hoped she had gotten away safely, knowing she had Bear with her and could easily defend herself, yet he had thought he could defend himself also, but now he was a captive. His thoughts turned inward, *I just hope she did get away and can find that army patrol, and get them back here in time, otherwise...*

White Skunk had laid claim to the two blacks of the Schmidts, one a stud the other a mare. Jared Schmidt had brought them west with a plan to breed the big horses but when White Skunk saw the animals, he wanted them both and chose the stallion for his warhorse. Little did he know the breed had been used as warhorses by the knights of old in Europe over two centuries past. The big stud stood as White Skunk grabbed a handful of mane and swung up to mount the horse that stood close to seventeen hands and weighed about a ton. He sat proudly, looking down at the other warriors as they waited for him to lead them to the village. Skunk pictured himself riding into the village as a great warrior astride the impressive animal as the villagers gazed at his magnificence. He grinned as he dug heels to the big horse and felt his power beneath him as the stallion stepped out with his fast gait, chin tucked toward his chest, neck arched and lifting his feet high and moving quickly.

The warrior leading the sorrel with Reuben, jerked the lead and pulled the little gelding around, almost unseating Reuben, but he clasped his knees tight and fought for balance, refusing to be dumped and tortured by the renegades. The trail twisted through the trees and at the crest of the broad-shouldered hill, it kept to the high line of the thickly timbered ridge. Although a game trail, it was an old trail, perhaps used by the ancients, for he saw two of the trail markers where a young sapling had been bent parallel to the ground and pointed the way of the trail. Not only were these used to mark trails, but they were also known as prayer trees, bent for prayer, and holding the prayers of the individual and lifting them heavenward for as long as eight hundred years. Now those saplings had grown and appeared to be distorted trees with contorted trunks, but they had been used by the ancients to mark the trails.

When he was captured, the natives had taken his belt with the holstered Remington pistol and hatchet and had also taken his Henry rifle, but his Bowie knife still hung in the sheath between his shoulder blades and beneath his buckskin tunic, but he could not get at it with his hands bound behind his back. He did his best to keep his shoulders back to prevent showing the bulge of his knife, but it was a struggle as he fought to keep his balance aboard the bony-backed sorrel.

They soon crossed a low saddle between two higher hills, dropped into a winding arroyo and followed it south until they came to a wide splash of white-barked quakies, and White Skunk left the draw and took to the trees, mounted a low ridge, and dropped to the other side. A well-traveled trail showed itself in the bottom of a long gulch and Skunk grinned and waved at his followers as he pointed up the gulch where the tops of several hide lodges clawed at the sky. On the west side of the vale, a small creek, known by some as Kerber Creek, chuckled its way as it wound through the willows and chokecherries, keeping to the south edge of the widening valley. Lodges were scattered across the narrow valley, extending west where another dry creek merged with the lower creek. Reuben guessed there to be about forty lodges stretched along this less than three hundred yards of creek bottom.

The returning party of about a dozen warriors was hailed by the villagers as they came near. Many of the people gravitated toward the returning men, most looking at White Skunk and his big black horse that seemed to relish the attention and lifted his big feet a little higher as he tossed his head about, the long mane flashing and bouncing as he moved. Skunk sat proudly, sticking out his chest and lifting Reuben's rifle high as he shouted his war cry.

The ruckus drew the attention of the village and brought the leaders from their lodges and from their places around the cook fires. A wide compound lay before a large bull hide lodge adorned with paintings and with ribbons flying from the smoke poles. A stoic figure stood before the lodge, a woman at his side and two other distinguished figures slightly behind him. Reuben recognized these as the leaders of the village, probably the head chief, his primary war leader, and the shaman.

White Skunk rode into the compound, reining his big black side to side, stopped him and swung his leg over the withers of the big horse and dropped to the ground. He turned, his rifle cradled in his arms across his chest and nodded to the chief, "Ho, Cuchutikay, we have returned! We have taken scalps of the white men," he waved the rifle with a scalp dangling from its fore stock, "weapons, horses, a captive, and other goods. We have shown these *kogöv(ü) kwichap(ü),* that the *Nuutsiu Kahpota* are great warriors!" The warriors behind him lifted their war cries at the praise. The leaders remained stoic, looking from Skunk to the others and the chief led his council as they walked among the stolen horses and the displayed bounty of their raids.

The medicine man, *Tuuwüchiich(i),* Black Bird, spoke quietly to the chief and the chief looked at Skunk. "We will talk," and walked back to his lodge. Skunk nodded, turned to his men, and began barking orders about the horses, goods, and the captive. Reuben was roughly pulled from his mount, dragged to the edge of the trees where he was bound with his arms pulled behind him and tied behind the trunk of an aspen. The bonds were loose enough, he slid to the ground and stretched out his legs as he leaned against the tree, looking into the village. He knew his treatment rested in the hands of the chief and his council, but until then, it appeared he was ignored by the villagers as they shared in the bounty of the stolen goods.

16 / PATROL

The mule ran free rein and was not about to let his friend, Blue, get away from him. Elly, aboard her spotted Appaloosa, was laying low on the neck of the little mare and trusting her to pick her own footing. The trail that followed the willow and aspen-lined creek in the bottom of the steep-sided arroyo, kept to the north slope just above the creek bottom. They were riding into the sun, but the sure-footed little mare missed nary a step, even though the trail often dropped to the creek when the steep slopes on her left pushed at the narrow trail. It was just over two miles of rough riding before the draw opened into the San Luis Valley. Elly reined up, pointed her mare to the blend of aspen and ponderosa at the mouth of the arroyo but stopped at the creek to let the animals take water. She went to one knee beside her Appy and scooped a couple handfuls of water as she watched Bear and the horses drink. Their sides were heaving and once watered, they lifted their heads to look at the valley, glanced down to Elly, and took another drink.

Elly stood and waded across the shallow stream,

leading the animals, and watched Bear roll his hide to shake off the water. She stepped into the shade of the pines and sat down, letting the animals crop a little grass, and as she looked at the empty valley, she shook her head, muttered a short prayer, and stepped back aboard the Appy. As they walked from the trees, Elly shaded her eyes and looked to the south. She was in the upper end of the big valley, and it was a good three day's ride back to Fort Garland. She shook her head, lifted her eyes heavenward, *Lord, help me find that patrol, let 'em be close and willing to help, Reuben needs us! Please Lord!*

She kept to the tree line, preferring the protection of the trees and hills to the open flat lands below, but keeping to the higher ground also gave her a better view of the open valley. Like most mountain valleys, the surrounding mountains had shed topsoil over the decades and eons as snowmelt and rainstorm runoff carried the soil from the high country to make broad alluvial plains on both sides of the valley. The rich soil also held better vegetation with grasses and berry bushes being abundant.

Elly was anxious and kicked the Appaloosa up to a canter then a gallop, the lead to Blue going slack as the long-legged roan stayed at the side of the Appy and the free rein mule to the far side of Blue. She twisted around to look at her back trail, saw the rising dust cloud and shook her head, but kept the pace. After less than a mile, she dropped to a canter, and slowed to a walk. Reining up, she dropped to the ground and walked to the head of her Appy, talking and occasionally stroking the horse's head, yet always watchful for any sign of life, Indian or cavalry.

Just shy of midday, she spotted the volcanic cone they had seen a few days earlier when Reuben had used the hilltop for one of his reconnoiters. She grinned at the remembrance, wishing she had his binoculars so she could have a look-see and hopefully spot the cavalry patrol. She also remembered this was where they had followed the other war party after they had attacked the freighter wagons, but Reuben said they rode south and around the point where the hills receded, and the valley widened. She looked at the peak, and a slow grin began to split her face. She pushed across the little creek and went to a cluster of cottonwood and scrub oak. Stepping down, she went to the packs on the mule and began digging in one of the panniers, muttered a "Yes!" and pulled out a tubular leather case. It was the encased brass telescope that had been a keepsake of her father's passed down from his father who was a seafaring man.

She tethered the animals and started her climb up the cone-shaped hill, angling across the north face and back to zigzag up the rather steep hill. Once atop, she seated herself on a big stone, took out the scope and stretched it out and began to focus on the distant flats. She turned to her right, scanned the mouth of the wide draw that held the creek below, then slowly turned to look at the timbered hills, the rolling flats, and the distant flatland of the massive valley. She moved the telescope to scan the wide-open land, moving it slowly as she saw a few deer near the stream in the bottom, a small herd of antelope grazing on the bunchgrass this side of the creek, and lifted the scope to the distant foothills of the Sangre de Cristos. Disappointed, she lowered the scope, looked at the dusty valley bottom, took a deep breath and more determined, lifted the scope for another scan. As she brought the scope back to the edge of the foothills directly south of her position, she paused when she thought she saw dust.

Coming almost directly toward her, a column of dusty blue-clad cavalry followed the banner of the Company I, 1st Colorado Cavalry. The red-and-white banner fluttered in the breeze and Elly watched for just a moment, turned away as she cased the telescope and started off the hill, digging heels as she lunged, slid, and skidded to the bottom of the steep hill. Quickly grabbing up the tethers of the animals and with Bear at her side, she swung aboard her Appy and reined her around as she slapped legs to the spotted horse to round the point and head off the patrol.

They came through a bit of a notch between a long ridge to the right and the shoulder of the cone hill on the left. Elly saw them coming, a thin dust cloud following, and waited a moment, then stood in her stirrups and lifted her hand high, grinning at the blessed sight. As they drew near, she recognized Lieutenant Edward Jacobs, the subordinate to the post commander, Captain Kerber. When he recognized her, the lieutenant lifted a hand to halt the column and ride forward, a crusty-looking sergeant beside him. "Well, Mrs. Grundy! We didn't expect to see you here." He looked beyond her, frowned, "And where is the marshal?"

Elly chuckled at his referring to Reuben as *the* marshal, little realizing or remembering she was also a deputy, but she answered, "Taken by some renegade Ute. That's why I'm here. I was lookin' for you and hopin' you'd help me get him back."

The lieutenant frowned, "Are you sure they were Ute?"

"Yes, led by a renegade named White Skunk. We ran into him before when we were with a family of settlers, run him and his men off, but they returned later and killed the family and took their goods. They also have some white outlaws and gold hunters ridin' with 'em."

"When was your husband taken?"

"This morning. He was scouting their camp, I heard a shot and shortly after, two of the Ute tried to take me, but Bear," nodding to her dog that stood close by, watching the soldiers, "and I took care of them, but not before they said they had Reuben and wanted me to go with 'em. I politely declined and came lookin' for you."

"What do you mean, you *took care of them?*"

"Killed 'em."

The lieutenant and the sergeant frowned as they looked at her and down at the dog. Sergeant O'Malley spoke to the lieutenant, "Sir, we were backtrackin' that party of Utes and I'm thinkin' they came from up Kerber Creek, yonder. Think maybe the camp of those renegades might be up there."

Elly shook her head, "If you were backtracking a band that went around that point sometime yesterday, that was another bunch. They weren't renegades, but they did attack some gold hunters in freight wagons, killed one, wounded a couple others, but we helped run them off and the gold hunters skedaddled down Poncha Pass."

"So, you're saying this was a different bunch than those that took your man?" asked the sergeant, scowling.

"Ummhmm. I don't know where the bunch of renegades was headin', but they're up another draw, a few miles back thataway," nodding to the north end of the valley.

"How many were in the bunch you call renegades?" asked the lieutenant.

"Maybe ten, give or take, and the three outlaws."

The sergeant leaned forward, turned to the lieutenant, and pointed to the narrow valley that carried Kerber Creek. "Sir, I know this country, I've hunted and chased Injuns all over it. That valley yonder bends back to the north and is on the backside of this line of foothills." He pointed to the long line of timber-covered mountains that sided the west edge of the valley. "Ever one o' these draws lead up to that long ridge yonder. If they was at the head of any o' these draws, and didn't come out down here in the valley, stands to reason they went o'er the ridge and dropped into Kerber Creek headwaters. Could be the main camp o' them Capote is up yonder ways."

"How far up thataway is the place you were camped?" asked the lieutenant, looking at Elly.

"Bout two, three miles this side of the crest of the pass. A narrow arroyo with lots of aspen in the bottom and a trail that sided the creek."

"I think I know that spot, and if I'm right, there is a trail o'er the top to Kerber Creek," offered the sergeant.

"Alright sergeant, you take second squad, that'll give you about fourteen men, and you follow up this creek," nodding to the creek in the bottom before them, "and I'll take the rest and we'll go with the lady here, and we'll follow that bunch. If you're thinkin' right, we'll probably meet at the camp of the Ute, if there is a camp," ordered the lieutenant.

"Lieutenant, thank you," replied Elly, reining her mount around to lead off and return to their previous camp and hopefully find Reuben.

17 / DISCOVERY

The bonds were chafing his wrists as he fought against the rawhide bindings. He was thinking of any way he could free himself, or at least get the knife from the scabbard at his back and cut the bindings. Reuben had been ignored for a while until he saw a man coming toward him. Reuben recognized him as the shaman or medicine man. With a quill vest in red and white, a porcupine roach standing high with three feathers behind a scalp lock, long braids hanging over his shoulders intertwined with beaver fur, fringed and beaded leggings and a breech cloth with beads and quills that matched the vest; he was an impressive figure. Walking with a purpose in his step, his stoic expression accented his broad forehead, high cheekbones, and square jaw that gave him a formidable appearance. He carried a long-handled war club with a scalp lock dangling from a beaded cord, and he glared at Reuben. Without a word, the man seated himself cross-legged before Reuben and looked at him, appearing to try to pierce his eyes with his stare. He lay his war club in his lap and began to speak, using sign and his talk. "I am

Tuuwüchiich(i), Black Bird, I am the Shaman of my people. Why are you here?" He spoke with a mix of English, Spanish, and Uto-Aztecan, the language of his people.

Reuben nodded, understanding most of what he said, although he did understand much of the Ute tongue, he was not very conversant in their language. He motioned with his head to the side, *"Nanama' waygay niyapö'"* which was his attempt at saying "We will talk with sign," as he nodded toward his shoulder, implying the freeing his hands.

Black Bird nodded, stood, and went behind the tree, quickly cutting the rawhide thongs that bound Reuben. The medicine man returned to his place and seated himself as before. As the man glared at him, Reuben began to explain, using sign and English interspersed with a few Ute words. "I first saw White Skunk when I was with a white family, a crippled man, a woman, and a boy. Skunk said they must leave, but I showed him what I would do if he and his men attacked when I shot the hat off a white man that was with his band." He continued to explain about leaving the family and that Skunk and his brave warriors later attacked, killed, mutilated the three, stole their horses and goods, and burned the wagon. He also added about the white outlaws that had joined White Skunk to find where he got the gold.

He continued, "I am a U.S. Marshal," taking the badge from his tunic pocket to show the man, "and I was after the white men. But I was taken by Skunk's men and heard him tell the white men about the gold and sent them to buy rifles. That is wrong by the treaty the Ute people have signed."

"This is the land of the *Nuutsiu,* and the whites are not to be here," countered Black Bird.

"I agree, but Ouray of the Tabeguache wants all the Ute people to join together and agree to ceding all this valley to the whites in exchange for many goods from the government."

"Hah! Ouray is wrong! His subchief, Shavano is here and asks our leaders to come to meet with him. Nicaagat of the Yapudttka, Ignacio of the Weeminuche, and Kaniache of the Mouache are to go to the fort to talk with Ouray and the white soldiers."

"My friend, Kaniache, does not want to make this treaty. He has vowed to fight it and not let the land of the *Nuutsiu* go to the whites. What will the others do?"

Black Bird frowned at Reuben, "You are a friend to Kaniache?"

"Yes, and his woman, Little Turtle, and his son, Running Elk. My woman and I were with Kaniache in the time of greenup. Kaniache and his people are good people, they do not attack crippled men, women, and children and claim a great victory as your White Skunk has done."

Black Bird snarled, spat to the side, "White Skunk was sent from our village. His return angers Cuchutikay. He was to bring meat to our people, but brings you, a few horses, and things that cannot be eaten. Our people are hungry, and he wants to make war!"

"What will your leaders do?"

"I come to hear from you what happened with the whites and why you are captive. This I will tell my chief." He started to rise and Reuben added, "When you speak to them, tell them I am a U.S. Marshal, and my woman has gone to the fort to bring many soldiers here for me. Skunk has brought you trouble."

"His men said Skunk sent two warriors for your woman, but they have not returned. She must be a good woman!" he chuckled as he turned away.

"She is a good warrior. Your men have not returned because they are dead! Killed by a white woman warrior!" Although he did not know this for certain, but he wanted to believe it to be so and needed these people to also believe.

Black Bird turned back to look at the man, motioned to two other warriors that had come from the lodges and stood watching, "You! When it is time, you will bring this man to the lodge of the council!" Bird looked back at Reuben, "You will tell the council what you have told me."

Reuben sat before the tall aspen, looked at the two warriors as they approached and watched as one pulled a long strip of rawhide from his belt and started to bind his wrists again, but was stopped by two women that came behind them, one carrying a platter of food, the other with a bladder of water. Reuben glanced to the sky to see the bright sun send long lances of gold to pierce the canopy of aspen leaves and looked back to the women who came near. Both women went to their knees before Reuben, neither with a frown or smile, but wary of the white man. The woman with the platter motioned for him to eat and sat back as Reuben placed the platter on his crossed legs. He nodded to the women, smiled, signed as he said, "I am Reuben, *Ta'wach(i) mamaka saagwagar(ü) kavaa,* or Man with Blue Horse. *Tuvwichi'ay,* I am thankful."

Both women smiled and relaxed to wait for him to finish. As he began, he spoke with the women, "Tell me about Senawahv." He knew Senawahv was the name for the Ute creator of the land, and he wanted to know what they believed.

"I am *Miipüch(i) wichich(i),* Little Bird. Senawahv is the creator of all things." She knew English, but she also used sign to answer. Her companion, White Crane, did not know English and Little Bird wanted her to understand what was said between them.

"The name we have for the creator is God and His son is Jesus Christ. In the beginning before there was anything, there was God and He made something out of nothing, creating all things, people, and animals. Our Bible tells us of this," began Reuben, taking his time consuming the delicious stew that filled the platter before him. The meat was tender and tasty, and he recognized some, but not all, of the vegetables that lay in the gravy. As he spoke, he took a few bites, looking from one to the other, smiling and listened to the women.

"Yes, Senawahv created all things and people. Our Shaman speaks to Senawahv to bring healing and help as it is needed."

"Do you speak to Senawahv?"

Both women frowned, looking to one another and to Reuben, "No, that is for the Shaman."

"We talk to our God ourselves. We do not need to wait for a Shaman or anyone else. God speaks to us through His book, the Bible, and tells us what we are to do, how we are to live and treat one another, and more."

Again, the women frowned, Bird asked, "What is this *Bible?*"

They spoke for a while as Reuben tried to explain about the Bible and the difference between God and Senawahv. Then he asked, "When you die, what happens to your *nuu'aa,* your soul or spirit? And what do the people do that do not die, you know, the family?"

The women spoke with one another, and Bird turned to Reuben, "We," motioning to herself and White Crane, "the family, grieve for a long time, cut hair, fast, mourn, until after the one that dies, his *nuu'aa* is gone."

"But what happens to the one that dies?"

"He goes where Senawahv sends him."

"Is that a good place or a bad place?"

"It is like this place," answered Bird, motioning around at the trees and more. "What does your God do to those that die?"

Reuben smiled, sat aside the empty platter, and leaned forward, "Our God, in His Bible, tells us about the place called Heaven, or *tugupaya.*" He went on to tell how the Bible describes the wonders of heaven, the difference from hell, and that the word of God tells us how we can know for sure that Heaven is our home. They were surprised to hear that anyone could talk to God and that anyone could do as the Bible says and be certain of Heaven.

"But what about those that are *üvüüni,* evil, like White Skunk?"

Reuben was surprised to hear the women speak of White Skunk that way, but it also told him of the lack of esteem his own people had for him. Reuben answered, "When God says that if anyone believes in their heart and truly calls on God for forgiveness, He will grant it and save him or her from an eternity in Hell. But if they don't really mean it, they just say the words but don't believe it here," he touched his heart, "then it will not happen. But God also says, no matter who the person is, if he means it, he will receive that gift of eternal life and know Heaven as his home. But more than that, when someone truly means it, they are made brand-new for when we are *in Christ, we are a new creation. Old things are passed away, behold all things become new!" (II Corinthians 5:17)*

The women looked at one another, nodded to one another, and Bird turned back to Reuben, "Can we do that? Ask for that free gift of eternal life?"

Reuben smiled, "Yes you can, now all you have to do..." and he explained about prayer and talking directly to God, then led them in the simple prayer to ask for forgiveness for their sin and grant them the gift of eternal life. They also added a request to learn more about God and his Bible. When they said "Amen," they looked at one another, broad smiles on their faces and the women hugged one another, turned to Reuben, and thanked him. Their excitement caused them to stand, grab up the platter and bladder, then trot off to tell others what had happened.

Reuben smiled as he watched, but his smile faded when the two warriors came close and started to bind his hands again, but were stopped when Black Bird called, "Bring him!"

18 / STRATEGY

The stench of death lay in the clearing that had been their camp. Elly nudged the Appaloosa mare through the trees, scattering the feathered carrion eaters, but the badger snarled, and the coyotes cowered as the crows and turkey buzzards took flight. Elly covered her nose and mouth with her neck scarf, turned in her saddle to watch the lieutenant and the cavalry men do much the same. Lieutenant Jacobs pushed his mount beside Elly, "You really *did* kill 'em!"

Elly nodded, pointing to the trees, "My husband went that way," indicating a dim game trail, "he was sure the renegade camp was just over that hill."

The captain nodded, turned back to his men, "Corporal Sandusky!" motioning the man forward. As he drew alongside, "The lady says her man, the marshal, took that trail. There might be a camp of renegades just over the top, scout it out. Do not engage!"

The corporal asked, "And if the camp is not there or the renegades have gone?"

"Find their trail, follow it, but leave sign for us."

"Yes sir!" replied the corporal, saluting. When the

salute was returned, he took to the trail and disappeared into the trees.

"We'll follow, but it'll have to be single file," stated the lieutenant, speaking to Elly. "I'll take the lead, ma'am."

"After you, lieutenant."

The lieutenant reined his mount around to face his men who had crowded into the clearing, scattering the carrion eaters into the trees although they could still be heard fighting over the scraps taken. The men looked to their commanding officer as he began, "Men, we're on the trail of a band of renegades that also have some outlaw white men with them. Not sure how many there will be, but if we encounter them before Sergeant O'Malley and the second squad make their way up the other draw, we'll have a fight on our hands. So, stay ready, move as quietly as possible, keep your eyes open, and no lagging behind. We'll need every man in this fight."

The men listened attentively, most of whom had seen very little action and the possibility of a fight stirred their emotions for this is what they had enlisted for, thinking they would go east to the war, but being stationed at Fort Garland hindered those thoughts. They looked at one another, grinning, and back to the lieutenant. The officer nodded, swung his mount around and started to the trees, motioned the men to follow.

The trail was narrow at best and the riders often had to sidestep branches, duck under limbs, and push aside saplings, but they soon crested the hill and with no sign of the scout, continued on the trail down the slight slope, spotting the clearings through the trees and the scout waiting in the open. When the lieutenant broke from the trees, the corporal saluted, "Sir! The renegades were camped here. The horses were in the upper clearing, the natives in the near one, and the white outlaws in the lower clearing. The whites left through there," pointing to the tree line on the upper end of the biggest clearing, "looks like they headed northwest down the draw. The natives took that trail," pointing to the obvious trail that split the trees but pointed uphill, "and I believe they had a bound captive with them. There were no boot tracks, other than the white men, but there was a captive bound with rawhide and lifted to a horse. They went south on a trail that follows the ridge, yonder," pointing over his left shoulder to the timbered hillside beyond.

"Good report, Corporal! Continue your scout, blaze a sign for us or mark the trail. If you spot something we need to know, wait for us."

"Yes sir!" replied the grinning corporal, saluting and swinging back aboard his mount. They watched him disappear into the trees and the officer turned to Elly, "You wouldn't know it, but that boy is part Osage and the best tracker in the outfit. Good man!"

He turned to his men, "Men, we'll take a short break here, let your mounts have a breather and get some water and graze. You break out your rations and do the same. We'll be leaving in about fifteen." His nod gave them the go ahead to dismount and take their break. He turned to Elly, "Ma'am, I'll have one of our men take care of your horses and mule, if you'd like."

"That's alright, lieutenant, I'll tend to 'em myself." She dismounted, loosened the girths on the horses and the mule, led them to the trickle of water on the upper edge of the clearing and tethered them within reach of grass, dropping in the shade herself with a pouch of pemmican in her hand. She leaned back against a big aspen, took a deep breath, and muttered a silent prayer as she glanced heavenward.

She looked up as the lieutenant came near. He nodded to the shade, "You mind?" suggesting he be seated nearby.

"That'll be fine, lieutenant." As he was seated, she extended the drawstring pouch with the pemmican, "Care for some pemmican?"

"Don't believe I've ever had any. Don't mind if I do." He pulled out a couple pieces, frowning, smelled it and took a tentative bite, lifted his eyebrows as he grinned, "Say, that's pretty tasty!"

Elly smiled, "Thank you. I made that."

The lieutenant looked at her and asked, "So, how is it you became a deputy marshal? I mean, after all, out here in the wilds with the natives, just you and your husband, and both of you marshals that are tasked with trying to keep the peace and more. Just doesn't seem fitting for a lady like yourself to be doing such a thing."

Elly chuckled, shook her head, and began explaining the past, from the time she met Reuben after he rescued her and the others from the Sioux to the appointment as marshals to help the Overland Stage Company and their continued duties as marshals. "I guess it's as much from the marshal's service being shorthanded in a time of war as us being in the right place at the wrong time!" she shrugged as she took another piece of pemmican and pulled the drawstring tight on the pouch.

The lieutenant chuckled, shaking his head, "And I joined the army for the adventure! Maybe I should have joined the marshal's service instead!"

They both laughed and the lieutenant stood, offered his hand to Elly and she stood. The officer looked toward the men now seated in the shade and lounging about, he made a circling motion over his head, whistled, and brought the men to their feet. Within moments, they were on the move following the trail of the ancients atop the timbered ridge to the south.

It was pushing toward late afternoon when the column met with Corporal Sandusky where he waited in the shade of some aspen at the lower end of a big grove that painted the wide swath of mountainside as it climbed to its crest. He stood, saluted the lieutenant, and waited for the officer to step down before he began his report.

He pointed to the aspen, "Right here's where the renegade band crossed over. Less'n a mile yonder on the other side of this line of foothills is a long basin with the creek that Sergeant O'Malley is followin' and there's about forty lodges of Ute camped there. I didn't get close enough to see much or to be seen. I come back here, went down the gulch there," pointing to the south, "where this gulch meets that creek yonder. I found the sergeant down there and he's waiting for word from you."

"Tell me about this trail and the village," encouraged the lieutenant.

"Well, sir, this trail, or whatever trail we follow or make, can stay in the trees well above the camp till we get around to the upper end. Then we can drop down any time. It's only 'bout a mile or so, even keepin' to the trees. Now O'Malley's about the same distance below the camp. So, the way I figger, we can head out 'bout the same time, and hit the camp together, us from above it, him below."

"I like the way you're thinkin', Corporal. Now, we'll need you to lead us through the trees an' such to get above the camp..." he paused, turned toward the men, "Smitty! Front and center!"

A man promptly slapped legs to his mount, reporting

to the lieutenant. He was an older man, grey showing at his temples, wrinkles on his brow, and laugh lines at his eyes and the corners of his mouth. His uniform sleeve showed evidence of sewn on and torn off stripes on more than one occasion, but the hash marks on the sleeve told of several years of service. The man sharply saluted the lieutenant and Jacobs began, "Smitty, you're goin' down the draw here and meet O'Malley. Tell him we're goin' over the hill here and approaching the encampment from the upper end. He's to follow the creek bottom and approach from the lower end. Tell him no shooting unless fired upon, but have the men in a line, weapons in hand, and approach slowly. We'll be doin' the same from above. Got that?"

"Yes sir, lieutenant, sir!"

"Also," he paused as he looked to the sun that was lowering in the west, gauged the time until it dropped below the mountain, looked at the man, "when the sun drops below the mountain yonder, start the approach!"

"Yes sir!"

"Move out then." He turned to the corporal, "Lead the way, corporal!" The corporal swung aboard his mount and started up the trail that split the aspen, followed close by the lieutenant, Elly, and the rest of the squad. As they moved through the trees, the lieutenant turned to Elly, "Pass the word to the men, we're close to the camp, move as quiet as possible!"

Elly nodded, twisted around in her saddle, and spoke to the man behind her, having to raise her voice a bit because of the pack mule and Blue that trailed behind her, but the man got the word and passed it along. Elly had heard the orders given to the scout and the other man and looked at the sun to see the golden orb cradled in the western mountains. It would be less than fifteen minutes until the sun dropped below the horizon and she looked through the trees, craning for a view of the village and saw a few of the tipis in the bottom of the narrow valley below. They were about a half mile above them, but the trees were thick enough to cover their approach. She shook her head, reached for her Henry, and slipped it from the scabbard to lay it across the pommel of her saddle, jacked a round in the chamber and slowly lowered the hammer. She breathed deep, looked at the lieutenant as he led the way behind the scout, and muttered a quick prayer.

19 / COUNCIL

Cuchutikay sat to the left of the entry of the lodge. He was in the place of honor for the council that was seated on either side. The shaman, Black Bird, was to his left, the war leader, a young man called Severo, was on Black Bird's left. To the chief's right, sat another leader of the *Nuutsiu(ü) Ute,* Shavano of the Tabeguache, a friend and subchief of Ouray. Other elders were seated on either side and behind the leaders. Reuben was shoved into the entry, stumbled as he fought for his balance, and stood, looking about, and at the motion of Cuchutikay, seated himself opposite the leaders, the empty fire ring between them. He noticed White Skunk sat to the far side, near others that appeared to be his warriors, all glaring at Reuben as he entered.

The stoic faces sat unmoving, watching, questioning, and doubtful. The chief began, using sign with his words, "Black Bird tells us you told of White Skunk and his attack on a white man's wagon." He paused, looking at Reuben, waiting for an answer.

"Yes, I told of what I saw and knew that happened."

"Tell this again."

Reuben looked around the circle, lowered his eyes to the fire ring, and began to tell of the events since his first time meeting White Skunk. When he told of the attack on the wagon, how White Skunk and his warriors attacked a crippled man, a woman, and a boy, mutilated the bodies and robbed them, White Skunk jumped to his feet and hollered, *"Tuvüchürü'ay!"* which is to say, "He lies!" but a glaring expression and slight movement of the hand of the chief, silenced him and he sat down, mumbling.

Reuben continued, telling of the attack on the freight wagons by the other Ute war party, and his return to the trail of White Skunk and the outlaw gold hunters. He added what Hickam, or Bear Face, had said about finding the gold and not buying the rifles as White Skunk wanted but leaving with the gold. He finished his tale, looked down at the fire ring and sat back, watching the chief and the other leaders.

For a moment, they talked among themselves, often gesturing, and appeared to be arguing, until the chief raised his hands and silenced the council. He spoke softly to the council, looked from man to man to see their decision as to what he said, then nodded. He looked to Reuben, "You are the captive of White Skunk. What he has done is without honor." He motioned to the two men that brought Reuben into the lodge, and they stood, motioned to Reuben to follow, and took him from the lodge.

As he stepped from the entry, the two men grasped his arms and led him to the tree where he had been tied earlier, dropped him to his haunches beside the tree and began tying him as before. They stood and turned away, but a commotion in the village caught their attention and they left in a hurry.

"Sir! The sun's 'bout gone!" reported Corporal Sandusky, looking from the last arc of the sun as it colored the western sky with shades of orange and gold, to the lieutenant, sitting astride his mount just inside the trees above the village. His voice was low, but the urgency in his words was evident.

"I see it, Corporal! Line 'em out!" he ordered, also in a quiet voice, yet making a wave of his arm to point to the trees at the edge of the little creek in the bottom of the draw. Using hand signals, the corporal directed the men to move through the trees, forming a mounted skirmish line across the arroyo above the village. With a glance over his shoulder to the disappearing sun, the lieutenant looked down the line and lifted his arm, giving the signal for the men to slowly move, keeping a line across the narrow vale, making their way toward the village.

The lieutenant was in the middle of the line, Elly beside him, and the line stretched out, seven men either side, evenly spaced. Each man with the butt of his rifle on his thigh, muzzle to the sky, hammer at full cock, and finger near the trigger. The men had .56-56 Spencer carbines that were new to the west, most provided to the soldiers in the war, but a recent shipment to Fort Garland equipped the men with the new repeaters.

The alarm was quickly spread when a woman came from the creek, heavy water bladders over her shoulders when she spotted the soldiers, shouted, dropped the water, and ran through the village, but was met by two warriors sounding the alarm that soldiers were also coming from the lower end of the village. The lieutenant and his men drew even with the first few lodges, and

Elly said, "Lieutenant, let me try something. If it works, it might save some lives. Could you stop your men here?"

"What're you going to do?" asked a frowning lieutenant, looking askance at the woman.

"You'll see, just give me a few minutes."

Lieutenant Jacobs lifted one hand high, motioning the men to stop. He glanced to Elly, nodded, and she nudged her Appy forward, leading the riderless but saddled roan, and trailing the mule who would not be separated from his friend, Blue. Elly lay her rifle across her pommel and started through the village, several warriors glaring at her, holding rifles or bows with nocked arrows at the ready, but making no move to stop her. Two women stood before a lodge, wide-eyed as they watched this blonde-haired white woman with the black wolf dog before her. Elly looked at them, used sign and a mix of English and Ute to speak, "Maykw(a)."

When they responded in the same way, Elly asked, "Man with Blue Horse was captured by White Skunk. Where is my man?"

The women looked at one another and pointed between two lodges toward the trees. Elly looked at them, stood in her stirrups and looked to the trees to see Reuben, bound and tied to an aspen. He saw her and quickly gave the call of the nighthawk and she grinned, relief showing on her face as she started through the lodges toward the tree. As she turned aside, she saw several warriors come from a large lodge on the upper end of an open compound and one man break from the others and start toward the tree where Reuben was bound.

Elly recognized White Skunk, saw him grabbing at his tomahawk at his belt as he started at a run toward Reuben. She slapped legs to the Appy, and the little mare dug heels as she lunged forward, but Elly saw she could not get to Reuben before White Skunk. He lifted his hawk, screamed his war cry, and charged toward the helpless captive. Elly dropped into her saddle, lifted the Henry, and squeezed off a quick shot and jacked another round into the Henry.

Skunk stumbled, grabbing at his chest, looked to see his hair-pipe bone breastplate shattered, blood painting the gold nugget, and he fell to his knees. Elly pulled alongside the renegade; fired another round into the man and continued jacking round after round into the chamber and as her anger flared, she shot him again as he glared up at her, and her Henry bucked again and again at the man on his knees. He looked up at her, anger and fear flaring in his eyes as blood spurted from his chest, side, and neck, covering his hands. He opened his mouth to speak, but blood came dripping from his lips as he gasped, choked, and fell on his face.

Several warriors came at a run, weapons raised, but a shout from the village stopped them. They turned as Cuchutikay, and Shavano strode toward them. The chief of the Capote glared at the warriors, "This man," spitting the words as he glared at the body of White Skunk, "has shamed his people. If you choose his way, you will be banished from our people!" He looked from one man to the other as he sought an answer from each one. Every man dropped his eyes, lowered his weapon, and started past the leaders to the village. But the chief stopped two men, spoke quietly to them, and turned back to Reuben as the two walked away.

The two chiefs looked at Elly as she sat on her Appy, rifle now across the pommel, then turned away and went to Reuben. Cuchutikay cut his bonds to free him and said to Reuben, "White Skunk has shamed our people.

Your weapons will be returned, and you will be free to go."

Reuben stood, rubbing his wrists, and nodded to the chief, extended his hand, and clasped forearms with the man, "You are an honorable man, Cuchutikay. I hope we will have peace between our people." He looked at the other man, "I understand you are Shavano, a friend to Ouray and Kaniache. The leader of the Mouache is a friend of mine, and I hope that one day you will count me as a friend to the Capote and Tabeguache." He clasped forearms with Shavano and accepted his weapons as they were brought by the two men who had ridden with White Skunk and had taken the weapons from Reuben.

Elly tossed the lead to Blue to her man, smiling broadly as she did, "We better hurry up and get back to the soldier boys before somebody does somethin' stupid and starts a war!"

Reuben swung aboard Blue, reined him around and the two rode side by side through the village, the pack mule trailing behind, and met the lieutenant, leading his men in a column of two, through the center of the village in a show of force. He stopped when he saw Reuben and Elly coming toward them, but the appearance of the two chiefs prompted him to step down and greet the leaders. Elly reined up beside the three, looked at the lieutenant and explained what happened. Jacobs looked at the chiefs, "I am honored to meet you, the great chiefs of the Capote and the Tabeguache," and extended his hand to shake. He explained, "We came to get the marshal there, but I see you have things well in hand. Perhaps we will see you at the fort. I understand Chief Ouray has extended an invitation to other chiefs of the Ute people to come for a council of peace, is that correct?"

Cuchutikay looked at the lieutenant, a scowl showing his disdain, "Shavano, the friend of Ouray and a chief of the Tabeguache, has come to ask us and others to come to that council. We will talk of this and decide soon. Perhaps we will visit the fort when we come."

"That would be good, Chief. I hope you do." Jacobs nodded, turned away and stepped into his saddle and with a hand motion to his men, continued through the village to meet Sergeant O'Malley and the rest of the cavalry. Reuben and Elly followed the soldiers, but as they passed White Crane and Little Bird, they stopped and Reuben told Elly of the women and their time together. Elly smiled, stepped down and embraced both women, "I hope we will see one another again soon, but not as a captive."

The women giggled, nodded, and Little Bird said to Reuben, "Will you bring us the book of God so we can know more?"

Reuben grinned, knowing the Bible would be of little use until they learned to read, but greater things had happened before and perhaps would again. He nodded as Elly stepped aboard her Appy and they waved their goodbyes as they rode from the village.

20 / OUTLAWS

The big, dusty brown, sow grizzly ambled across the creek, swatted at the water—probably swiping at a tempting trout, stepped up on the bank, rolled her hide to shake off the water and bellied down in the sun-drenched grass. Elly shook her head and looked at Reuben, "Now what?"

Reuben chuckled, "Well, we're not sure where the outlaws are, upstream or down," he paused, shaded his eyes to look to the sun, "and it's pushin' noon, so, mebbe we should find us a shady spot, fix a little coffee and have us some vittles, and maybe even a short nap. She," nodding toward the grizz in the creek bottom less than a hundred yards away, "will prob'ly leave soon. As long as the wind doesn't change and these horses get a strong whiff, we'll be alright, but just to be safe, let's move a little further upstream and away from that big girl."

"Suits me! Far as I'm concerned, we're already too close!"

They were at the confluence of Poncha Creek and a smaller creek that came from the south. The bear had chosen the west side of Poncha Creek for her sunny nap, and Reuben and Elly were on the east side of the smaller creek, but neither stream was obstacle enough to prevent the sow from getting to them or their horses if she suddenly had a hankering for fresh meat. The smaller creek was thick with beaver ponds and willows, with the steep slope of the timbered hills showing more gnawed stumps than trees. Reuben pushed toward a cluster of aspen that sided the creek, seeing a grassy flat amid the white-barked, leafy trees. He stepped down, looked back down the creek, and satisfied, offered a hand to Elly to help her to the ground. Bear stood looking at their back trail, probably getting the scent of the grizzly for he stood with one paw lifted, head high and unmoving. A low growl rumbled as he looked back at Reuben but turned back quickly to watch downstream.

On the far side of Poncha Creek, the valley bottom was narrowed by the bald face of a steep-sided hill that stretched along the west edge of the creek into the long, narrow valley that carried the trickling stream. The finger of timbered hills that parted the streams stood tall with its black slopes rising abruptly from the narrow arroyo where beaver slapped their tails in warning of unwelcome visitors. The sun was high in the sky, unhindered by any clouds, leaving the azure sky as a backdrop for Old Sol. Reuben went to Bear's side, dropped his hand to the scruff of his neck, and spoke softly, "Is that grizzly still there, or has she moved off?"

As they watched, the big sow rose, shook, and ambled beside the creek, head swinging side to side as a scruffy furred cub came from the wills and they moved away, unafraid of anything or anyone for she was the biggest beast in the land and believed herself to be the top of the food chain. As they watched, the bear stopped, lifted her head and with nose in the air, slowly moved side to side. She rose to her hind feet, looking beyond the stream into the trees, took an awkward step as she turned to face the hillside, then dropped to all fours, swatted at the rambunctious cub and crashed across the stream, giving chase to some unseen game, and disappeared on the far side of the hill.

Reuben grinned and stroked Bear's head and neck, "Looks like she's gone for now, boy! Let's get us some food, shall we?" He noticed Bear had visibly relaxed and stood with tail wagging, tongue lolling, and a big grin on his face as he looked at Reuben. The dog followed him back to the clearing where Elly was just putting the coffeepot beside the little fire.

She looked up and smiled, "So, did the grizz leave?"

"Ummhmm, looked like she got a whiff of something that caught her interest and she and her cub disappeared into the trees the far side of that ridge yonder," answered Reuben, nodding toward the finger ridge that divided the streams.

"She had a cub?"

"Ummhmm," answered Reuben, grinning at his woman that always had a soft spot for any of the wilderness babies.

"So, you still think those outlaws are further up this creek?"

"Yeah, I do," answered Reuben, dropping to his haunches and watching as Elly dropped a handful of coffee into the pot. "I think we'll find sign of 'em soon. I overheard White Skunk when he told Hickam where he found that big nugget that he had hangin' 'round his neck, and near as I can figger, it's close to the headwaters of this creek," nodding toward the chuckling stream below them.

"Do you think it's much further?"

"Don't rightly know, could be just around the bend yonder, or five or ten miles upstream. We'll hafta be right careful, but we haven't seen any sign of 'em headin' back to the settlement, so..." he shrugged, setting the coffeepot back from the fire to let it settle. Elly lifted the lid, poured just a tad of cold water into the pot to hasten the settling of the grounds as both fell silent, pondering what might lie ahead.

"Look! I got some flakes!" shouted Pork, lifting his pan chest-high and pointing. He was standing in water almost knee-deep, his trousers soaked to his waist, but his grin was almost ear to ear as he shouted, pointing, looking at Hickam and Freckles. The two men, one upstream from Pork, the other building a rocker box on the bank, turned to face the shouter. "I got flakes!" he called, lowering the pan to look and count, he mumbled a moment, "Sixteen of 'em! It's a honey hole!" pointing to the backwater behind the big boulder that parted the waters midstream.

"Keep pannin'!" shouted Hickam, "We'll foller it upstream till we find the source!"

The long, lanky Freckles ran wet fingers through his carrot top hair, shaking his head, "I got a few flakes in the last pan, but ain't seen any in this'n!"

Hickam looked from Freckles to Pork, "Wal, he's in that backwater of that big rock, the current washes in behind it and leaves the gold." He stood, stretched, looked up and down the stream, "There," he pointed to another large stone that pushed the little stream away from the grassy bank, "try there, behind the rock where the current runs, like Pork's got. Mebbe there'll be more there."

This was the third day at the stream for the three men, with Hickam bossing the other two and had yet to get wet as he worked building a rocker box. They had found color on the second day and the further they moved upstream, the more promising it became. Hickam was convinced that the gold flakes in the stream came from a single source, the mother lode, that was somewhere upstream and probably hiding in the rocky slopes of the mountains. If they could find the source, they could be rich. He grinned and chuckled as he watched the long-legged Freckles splash his way up the stream, eager to try the new spot, hopeful of more flakes. Although they had already accumulated some gold, maybe a couple ounces, they had yet to find the real hot spot, the mother lode that every gold hunter dreamed about.

The men were upstream from several beaver ponds, working in the narrow confines of a steep-walled canyon. To their right, the north canyon wall was a steep limestone cliff that rose over seven hundred feet to top out on a shoulder of the larger mountain that capped a long ridge bearing black timber and stands of quakies. On their left, the steep but sparsely timbered shoulder of a granite-peaked mountain rose above timberline to show its bald head standing among the tall peaks. But the narrow-walled canyon pushed at the gold hunters, the stream cascading through the narrows and making their panning difficult. Hickam commandeered a narrow grassy flat for his workspace as he fashioned their rocker box, but the two underlings labored in the cold water, driven on by tidbits of gold flakes that teased their imaginations.

"I'm gonna take the horses and mules upstream and picket 'em on some grass. There's a patch near them beaver ponds," declared Hickam, standing, and stretching as he looked down at his crudely fashioned box.

"If'n you're doin' that, how 'bout puttin' on some coffee. Me'n Freckles been wadin' in this crick so long, I can't feel muh feet no more! We need to be warmin' up!" shouted Pork, fingering the silt in his pan.

"You just keep pannin' till we find that vein in these here mountains! We ain't gonna get rich on those measly flakes you're gettin'!" answered Hickam, walking past the rotund figure in the water. In their hurry to get to the stream, they left the animals tethered in the trees at the mouth of the canyon and Hickam went to the side of his gelding, reached for the rawhide tether but the horse jerked back, pulling the tether taut. A roar that shook the trees, bounced off the walls of the canyon, turned Hickam on his heels. The big silvertip grizzly stood tall, clawing at the air with his massive paws, cocked his head to the side, mouth wide, teeth bared, slobbers flying, as he let loose another protest at the strange intruders to his domain.

Hickam horse's eyes were wide, and he fought the lead, digging his heels to back away and jerking his head to the side to see behind him. Hickam grabbed his rifle from the scabbard as he snatched at the lead, pulled it free and stepped to the others as the big bay spun around and took off up the canyon. The other animals, quickly freed by Hickam, followed the gelding, all fleeing at a run. Hickam sidestepped, his Springfield rifle at his side, watching the big grizzly that stood at least eight feet tall. The frightened man searched frantically for an escape, but the bear had dropped to all fours, and swinging his head side to side slowly approached, a low growl rolling from his chest. Black eyes watched his prey, slobbers dripped from his mouth, big teeth crawled from under the snarled lip, and Hickam stutter stepped backward, raising the Springfield to his shoulder, bringing the hammer to full cock. Hickam's eyes showed white, he heard a scream, not realizing it was his own voice that screeched, and fought to keep a clear sight on the big bear's head. He jerked at the trigger, felt the hammer fall and rocked back on his heels as the long rifle bucked and blasted. The smoke from the muzzle clouded the narrow space, but Hickam turned to run, had his feet swatted from under him as the big bear, showing blood on one shoulder, rose to his hind feet, snarling down at the figure below him. Hickam crabbed back, screaming, crying, and shaking one hand at the bear as if he could keep the monster at bay with a waving hand.

The roar that came from the beast bounced across the narrow canyon, the screams of the terrified man doing little to harmonize with the chorus of terror. "NO! NO! NO!" came the staccato cries of horror, but the sudden blast of gunshots rattled the loose rocks high above the sheer cliff face, bouncing little stones and gravel to the creek bottom hundreds of feet below. The usual melodic chuckling of the mountain stream that made music with the clarion calls of mountain birds was drowned out with the cacophony of fear. Shouts from the two men that had grabbed their rifles from the narrow, dry creek bank when the horses and mules stampeded past, added to the melee and more shots came from the Spencer rifle in the hands of Freckles.

The big bear, distracted from his helpless prey, had turned to flee, blood showing on his silvertip fur, but he showed no signs of serious wounds, only occasionally slapping at the bloodspots as if swatting a pesky bug. He ambled away without so much as a glance over his shoulders and disappeared around the point of rocks at the end of the ridge.

Freckles went to the bloody figure on the ground, saw the terrified eyes watch him draw near and heard Hickam cry with a horrified voice, "Is he gone?"

"Yeah, he's gone," answered Freckles, looking down at the big man. The carrot-topped helper frowned as he shook his head and stepped closer. Hickam had messed himself, and the stench added to the smell of the bear and the fresh blood that came from Hickam's leg. The bear had broken Hickam's leg when he swatted at the fleeing man, knocking his feet from under him. Long claw marks showed, blood flowing from the wounds, the ripped britches hung in rags and soaked up the blood.

Freckles turned to Pork who stood staring wide-eyed, "Get me somethin' to bandage him with!"

"What!? Ain't nuthin' here. The mules done ran upstream and it'll take a while to catch up to 'em, and that's if the packs're still on 'em."

"Then go get 'em! I'll see what I can do for him till you get back." Freckles stood, holding the back of his hand to his nose and mouth, and looked at Hickam, "You stink!" He turned away as Pork took off at a trot, going after the animals. Freckles went to the edge of the creek, grabbed up a handful of mud and some grasses, jerked at some little willows and pulled a few free and returned to tend to the injured Hickam.

21 / DISCOVERY

The whiskey jug sat within reach of Hickam as he watched Freckles and Pork digging at the base of the limestone cliffs. The flakes of gold had petered out at where the base of the rocky cliff pushed the stream away. What appeared to be a thin vein of gold showed in the quartz outcropping that proved to be a larger vein of quartz that split the hard rock wall. The first bandage fashioned by Freckles had been a mud pack held in place by the big leaves of plantain, but after splinting the broken leg, the wound had been washed clean, whiskey splashed over the claw marks, and a fresh poultice of the plantain leaves was now held in place with a swatch of buckskin. Hickam kept the pain at bay with copious amounts of whiskey that were rapidly diminishing their supply.

Their camp was less than a half mile upstream where the animals were picketed, and their gear was stashed in the trees. The valley widened out, the stream meandered, and the beaver had made many ponds that were plentiful with brook trout, providing the men with ample food without taking time out to hunt for meat. Although

Hickam was of no help, he insisted on being near to watch the progress and give his orders to ensure his control.

Freckles and Pork stood on either side of the quartz deposit, each with a pickaxe, alternating swings and strikes, slowly chipping away at the crystalline-like stone. Each strike breaking away a chunk of quartz, and subsequent drags of the broad blade removed the debris from the deepening hole, but not before each piece was carefully examined by one or the other of the laborers. "Here! Here! Throw me a piece o' that rock!" ordered Hickam, holding out a hand ready to catch the fist-sized stone. Pork complied and lifted his pick for another swing. As the pieces of quartz showed flecks or veins of gold, those pieces were tossed into a pile on the bank of the creek near where Hickam sat, examining each piece. The men were focused on their work, Hickam intent on his inspection of each piece, and as greedy men are prone to do, they were oblivious to everything around them.

"WAIT!"

Freckles and Pork froze at the shout from Hickam, turned to face him and saw him lifting the largest of the rocks and pointing as he grinned and nodded.

"Did you see this!?" he shouted, "C'mere!"

The pair dropped their pickaxes, splashed from the water to the side of Hickam and looked at the stone. A gold vein, thicker than a man's thumb, twisted its way through the white crystal.

"This is it! We just gotta keep diggin'! The deeper you go, the bigger the vein!"

Reuben crabbed back from his promontory, hung his rifle over his shoulder by the sling and started back to a waiting Elly. He pushed through the pines, careful to choose his steps in the pine needle trail, moving quietly yet quickly. Elly watched as Reuben came from the trees, Bear came to his feet and stood, head high, tail wagging. Elly dropped her hand to Bear, looked at her man and asked, "So?"

"Spotted 'em. They're digging for gold at the base of that big cliff. I wasn't close enough to hear, but the big one, Bear Face or Hickam, had a splint on one leg and was sittin' off by himself but he appeared to be barkin' orders to the other two."

"Can we get to them? Take 'em?" asked Elly, sitting back on the rocks behind her as she looked at the frowning expression of her man.

"No, where they're at, the canyon is narrow, they're by the cliff face and there's no cover to get close enough. I think their camp might be further upstream, nothing shows downstream from where they're working. Maybe as it gets darker, they'll give up and go back to their camp, then..." he shrugged.

They were in the thick timber on the flank of the tall peak that terminated a long ridge that fell from the high-peaked mountain. The same mountain that was the north face, or south side, of the long canyon and stretched a good two miles to the headwaters of the little creek. The north side was a pair of lesser mountains, thicker timbered, but no less passable. There was no circumventing the canyon to try an approach from upstream of the outlaws' camp. They talked about the possibilities and decided to wait for nightfall and the movement of the men before they tried to form a plan to take the three into custody for their robbery of the trader Burnett and Hickam's part in the raid that killed the Schmidts.

The thick timber atop the slight shoulder that fell from the big mountain, gave way to a cluster of aspen that invited the couple into the slight clearing and grassy knoll. Reuben had spotted the site from below and led them into the site which was secluded and hidden from below. He stepped closer to Elly, took her in his arms and drew her close, causing her to lean into his caress but lift her face up to him, a slight squint to her eyes as she asked, "Alright, what are you up to?"

"I'm just grateful to you for always being by my side and for going after the soldiers when the Ute had me. We've been on the trail of these outlaws and movin' so fast, we haven't had time to enjoy being together."

Elly smiled, shook her head slightly and answered, "Uh, since we still don't have them in custody, it doesn't appear we have that time yet!" Her hands rested on his forearms as she looked at Reuben, "But why do I get the feeling there's more to this than just saying thanks?"

"I was thinkin' about asking you to stay back in camp again."

"Uh-uh, I'm not letting you do that again. You can go have your look-see, but you will not be leaving me in camp again! I'm gonna be right by your side or close by at least, whatever we have to do to take them down, but don't ask me to let you take off on your own again!" She dug her fingers into his arm to let him know she would hold on and not let go.

"Alright, alright. I understand, but we ain't doin' nothin' without some coffee."

Elly smiled and pulled back, turned to the pack mule, pulled the coffeepot from the pannier, and grabbed the canteen to fill the little pot. Reuben relaxed and grabbed some rocks to make a fire ring, broke some dead branches from the nearby spruce and shortly had a small fire going under the long branches of the spruce, letting the thin spiral of smoke dissipate in the needles. Reuben looked to the sky, guessed there to be about two hours of daylight left, and leaned back to relax with his wife.

"White Skunk said they were women! He was right—they have shown themselves women of the white men!" growled Big Thunder as he glared at Creeping Bear and Red Horse. He spoke of the leaders of the Ute people, Cuchutikay, Ouray, and Shavano, that had allowed the soldiers of the white men to enter their village and take the captive white marshal from them, after his woman had killed their leader, White Skunk. The three men had been with White Skunk when he sought to gain warriors in his efforts to drive the white men from the land of the *Nuutsiu(ü).* They were his first followers and had been with the former war leader as they fought the white settlers, but when White Skunk took the white gold seekers into their band, Big Thunder spoke against them, and was put down by White Skunk.

Thunder was angry; angry that Skunk had been killed and the woman who shot him was not killed. He was angry because he had been with White Skunk when they had captured the white man, and it was Thunder who had taken his weapons and claimed them as his own. He was angry because chief Cuchutikay demanded the weapons be returned to the white man. Thunder looked from Creeping Bear to Red Horse, "The white man, Bear Face, went to the place of the yellow stone and told White Skunk he would use the yellow stone, what they call gold, to get rifles. I do not trust any white man, they all lie and steal our land and our women, but they have great weapons. We could find this Bear Face and get rifles. If he does not get them from the white traders for us, we can take the weapons he and his men carry. With those, we can take more from the white traders and those that come into our land!"

"But Cuchutikay has said if we go the way of White Skunk, we will be banned from the village of our people!" pleaded Red Horse.

"How can we go the way of White Skunk when he is dead? If we do nothing and the white man takes our land, our people will die and there will be no village! If we drive the white man away, we will be honored and other warriors will join us as we destroy all white men!" growled Big Thunder, glaring at the two men that stood before him. "We need more warriors who believe as we do. You know those that rode with us and White Skunk, we must seek them out, tell them to join us, and others that may come." Red Horse and Creeping Bear looked to one another, nodding and agreeing with Big Thunder. "Go! Tell them we will leave before first light. We will go to where the white men seek the yellow stone! Then we will go to the white trader and get weapons for all our warriors! We will also find the white man and his woman who killed White Skunk and show them the *Nuutsiu(ü)* are great warriors that do not allow the stinking white men or their women to come into our land and kill our people!" Creeping Bear and Red Horse lifted their hands high to salute the memory of their leader and to show their alliance with Big Thunder.

The big moon hung high in the heavens, its bright orb masked by the shadowy clouds that stretched across the eastern sky, some hiding the lanterns of the night, others making the sky appear as a massive black shadow that held foreboding warnings. The narrow draw was sided by rocky outcroppings and scattered juniper, but the riders that saw themselves as great warriors determined to drive the white men from their land, made their way up the sandy bottomed creek bed. The finger of rock pushed aside the draw, forcing the riders to turn back on themselves and take the bend around the point where Big Thunder waited with Red Horse and Creeping Bear. Ten warriors came to join them, most familiar faces that had ridden with White Skunk before and some young men seeking warrior status among their people. Nothing was said, nods were given by the three that waited, as they mounted their horses and started up the long draw. Thirteen warriors, renegades all, choosing to follow the ancient way of warriors and reclaim their land, bring retribution upon the invaders of their territory, and restore the way of their people to their world.

22 / RETRIBUTION

"We gotta make this bigger if'n we wanna go any further!" shouted Pork, coughing and kicking, trying to get air, his upper body deep in the hole. He was using a mattock or small pickaxe to break up the quartz to get at the vein of gold, but the dust and cramped space was taking its toll.

"What'd you say?" whined Freckles who was dragging the rocks and dirt from behind the rotund form of Pork, adding more dust to the hole where the men had been working.

Pork started grumbling, kicking, and twisting his way back from the depths of the dusty hole. Freckles backed away, grabbed Pork's foot, and pulled to help his friend make his exit. As Pork came into the daylight, he waved the dust away from his face, spat, growled, and struggled to stand, coughing with every move. Bent over at the waist, hands on knees, he spat and choked trying to get some air in his dust-filled lungs. He looked at Freckles, turned to see Hickam seated in the shade of the single tree below the cliff face, shook his head and growled,

"That hole's gotta be bigger, ain't 'nuff room to swing the mattock, and if I get in a good swing, there's so much dust, I cain't breathe!" He looked up at the lanky Freckles, "Mebbe you can do it!"

"Nuh-uhn, can't do no holes like that! Gives me the heebyjeebs!" whined Freckles, shaking his head and stepping away from the hole. The diggings had bored into quartz-veined rock beneath a larger overhang and the two had pushed into the formation about five feet, always chasing the elusive spiderweb vein of gold. Whenever the vein seemed to peter out, the next strike of the mattock pick would break loose a good chunk of quartz and reveal another glimmer of vein and the elusive gold.

Pork stomped his feet and slapped at his trousers and shirt, making a cloud of dust that prompted him to move the short distance to the stream and splash into the water, dropping his face to the current to wash the dust from his hair and neck. He came up suddenly, swinging his head side to side to rid himself of the water, and wiped his face and neck with his hands and turned to look at the other men. He shook his head again and stomped from the water. With hands on hips, he looked at Hickam, "So, how much we got?"

"Ain't 'nuff! There's more there and a little more diggin', we'll be set with a good stake that'll see us where we wanna go!" answered the bear-faced man. He had been busy picking at the chunks of quartz to remove the pieces without any gold showing, trying to make their load less, and the better the percentage of gold to rock, the better the price for the ore. He lifted one to let the morning sun shine directly on the stone, turning it to see the vein and grinning as he held it up for the others to see.

"An' whar's that?" asked Pork.

"Wherever we want!"

Pork looked at Freckles, "So, I do all the work, you two just break 'em up, and…and…wal, I'm tired o' doin' it all! Mebbe I should get a bigger share?"

Freckles and Hickam looked at one another and Hickam looked to Pork. "Now Pork, if'n I could, I'd be in there doin' my share, but," he slapped his thigh, "this hyar leg won't let me!"

"Humph," mumbled Pork, looking from the stack of ore beside Hickam and back to the hole. "I don' like it!"

"What if we blasted it out?" asked Freckles, looking from Pork to Hickam.

"What'chu mean?" asked Pork.

"We got us a cask o' powder in that stuff we took off the trader, thot it'd be good tradin' to the Injuns fer them ol' flintlock rifles they got, but we din't have a chance to do no tradin'. What if we put that in thar and blast that rock loose? Then all we gots to do is drag it out, break it up, and head fer the assay office up to South Park!" He looked from Pork to Hickam and back.

"That pro'ly do it!" answered Hickam. "Yeah, they was doin' that all the time up yonder, them other fellas 'round Buckskin. They was blastin' everything!"

Pork looked from one to the other and mumbled, "I'm fer anything that makes that diggin' easier!" He looked at Freckles. "You go git it, I'll make a hole fer it!" He turned toward the hole, mumbling, "If'n I thot I'd hafta do so much work fer it, I'da never joined up with 'em. Coulda filed me a claim and done all the diggin' and kept all the gold!"

"What're you mumblin' about?" called Hickam.

Pork didn't answer, just grumbled and growled as he

grabbed the mattock and dropped to his knees to crawl into the hole.

Reuben twisted around to find a more comfortable position. He was belly down underneath a sizable spruce that stood at the base of a talus of slide-rock. The slight shoulder gave him enough of a promontory and the trees offered ample cover for him to watch, unseen, the diggings of the three outlaws. By line of sight, he was a little over a hundred yards from the hole at the base of the cliff, and his camp was less than a hundred yards behind him on the timbered shoulder where Elly waited with the horses and the big dog. They thought the outlaws would go to camp when dark fell, but they used candles and continued digging into the night, prompting Reuben to return to camp with Elly. Now it was approaching midmorning and the men had been digging for several hours.

Reuben moved the field glasses up and down the narrow draw, searching for the trail and any game trail that would afford access to the near side, or upstream from the diggings, but found none. With the narrows below the cliff and the sparsely timbered steep slope of the mountain on the near side, there was no way of approaching the outlaws with any cover. Any approach would be seen more than two hundred yards down the draw. He moved the glasses back on the trio as two of the men stood outside the diggings and one splashed into the water. Reuben chuckled as he watched, waiting to see what would happen for it appeared an argument was simmering just below the surface. He knew anytime unscrupulous characters join together in any illegal or immoral activity, the jealousy, greed, and short tempers always make for an argument at best, or a bloody battle at the worst.

The big black dog that had been their constant companion, slipped quietly beside Reuben, crawling on his belly just like the man. He felt the soft touch on his lower leg and the whispered voice of Elly said, “Anything happening?”

Reuben smiled, let a slight chuckle escape as he said, “Nothin’ new. They’re arguing a mite, no fightin’ yet, but…”

“I see what you mean about the narrow draw. What with the cliff on one side, slide-rock on the other, and the creek in the middle, there’s no way to get close enough to get the drop on ‘em and them not fight back or run off ‘fore we could get ‘em,” surmised Elly, moving down alongside of her man, peering through the tree branches to see the activity below.

Reuben handed over the binoculars and Elly squirmed around until she was comfortable with the field glasses, elbows on the ground, glasses to her eyes, as she adjusted her field of vision to see the outlaws. She frowned as she watched and narrated for Reuben, “The tall skinny one just came back and dropped to the hole, he’s sayin’ somethin’ to the man inside. Now he’s handing him a cask, looks like gunpowder.” She frowned, watching and handed the field glasses to Reuben, “What’re they gonna do?”

Reuben had a quick look as Freckles handed the cask into the hole, scooting it past the extended legs of Pork. “That size of cask will blow that place to kingdom come! They sure don’t know what they’re doin’ with that much powder.” He lifted his glasses to the rock face above the overhang, slide-rock and a rocky escarpment bigger than a house hung precariously overhead. He shook his head, "They're so blinded by greed for gold, they're not thinkin'!" As he watched, Freckles stood and moved back, watching Pork scuttle back from the big hole. Pork moved on hands and knees, laying a thin trail of powder from the cask inside, and out the opening. He had his neckerchief holding the powder and he carefully used both hands to lay the thin trail. Although Reuben could not see the powder, it was evident by their movements, what they were doing.

Pork stood, looked to Freckles and Hickam, slapped his hands together and dug in his shirt pocket for a lucifer. He waited a moment for Freckles to get further away, watched Hickam struggle with his sapling crutch and when the two men stood between two trees, the only two on that side of the creek below the cliff, and signaled, he struck the lucifer, let it flare up, and with another glance to his friends, he bent and started the powder burning. He watched it for just a moment, then turned and ran to join his friends.

Smoke trailed the line of burning powder, billowing out of the hole, and within moments, the hump of dirt, stone, and debris that lay atop the slight overhang, humped up as if lifted by the hair, dust puffing, and the blast from the powder keg shot from the hole like cannon fire. Smoke, dust, rocks, and more belched from the prospect hole, the overhang lifted, cracked in the middle, and dropped as if the giant of the mountains smashed down with the heel of his massive foot. The face of the escarpment and cliff let loose and slipped as if the massive stones were one, but as it tilted, long slabs, huge boulders, and shoulders of loose dirt and stone seemed to find their own way and began crashing down, dust billowing and thunder roaring and racketing off the steep walled canyon.

Reuben and Elly watched, mesmerized at the sight of something so solid, cracking and crashing, splitting into shards, slabs, and shafts—all driving and sliding down from the face of the mountain. The roar would have silenced even the thunder of the mountain storms as every bounce of a rock, split of a slab, strike of a stone, was magnified as the sound bounced back and forth across the narrow gorge. Reuben looked for the men, saw them running and diving for cover, the makeshift crutch of Hickam tossed aside as he scrambled for his life, each cascading boulder a cannonball chasing death and injury before it. Boulders bounced across the canyon floor, crashing into the thick timber, laying trees flat before them, others dammed the creek, muddying what water remained or found its way past the battle of boulders.

And silence fell, interrupted intermittently as each loosened stone sought release and bounded to the bottom. Dust clouds billowed, caught the wind, and drifted down canyon. High above, a golden eagle circled, looking at the destruction below. Perched atop the limestone cliff, a yellow-bellied marmot sat on his haunches, forefeet dangling at his chest, as he whistled a belated warning. Dust settled over the treetops, giving the dark green of the spruce and fir a shady grey cast.

Reuben searched the bottom for any sign of life of the three men, saw Freckles stand and use his hat to slap at his britches and shirt, ridding himself of the dust. He bent down to help Pork to his feet, and both men looked back at Hickam as he crawled from under the branches of the lone ponderosa pine. Water was already backing up from the rock-strewn dam, and Freckles and Pork walked into the cool water, splashing about and scooping water to their faces and necks. As they came from the water, Hickam said something to them, but they turned away and started upstream to their camp.

Reuben rolled to his side to look at Elly, started to say something but looked past her, frowned, and lifted his binoculars. He breathed deep, whispered, "Indians!"

23 / REPRISAL

The thundering roar racketed through the narrow canyon, spooking the horses and their riders. A quick glance to the sky expecting to see storm clouds instead showed a clear blue canopy. The men looked to one another, trying to bring their mounts under control as they skittered side to side, wide-eyed and nervous. As the horses were settled down, Big Thunder called, "Müwa'ni, Paga'nich(i), go, scout!" motioning the two warriors to the dim game trail that took to the dark timber.

The trail hung on the steep-sided mountain and pushed through the timber. It broke into the open at the bottom of a long and wide slide area, dropped toward what had been the willows and chokecherry bushes beside the creek, but now was a jumble of chunks of limestone, boulders, and rocky debris. The scouts dropped from their mounts and started across the rock-slide, picking their way carefully on the teetering slide-rock, leading the horses behind. The creek bottom was piled high with slide-rock from the limestone cliffs and rocky escarpments and a thin cloud of dust still wavered in the breeze of the deep draw.

Big Thunder and the other warriors stepped down and stood at the edge of the trees, looking down upon the grey waters of the trickling creek, the water flow less than it had been just moments before. The men talked among themselves, speculating on the cause of the thunder from the canyon.

Reuben watched as two of the warriors took to the trees, appearing to follow the trail that would side the creek below. He scanned the remaining warriors as they dismounted, and spoke softly to Elly, "I recognize a couple those warriors. One who's giving orders is the same one that took my weapons and at the orders of the chief, returned them, and he wasn't none too happy about it. Looks like these are prob'ly those that had followed White Skunk and are trying to pick up the banner, even after the chief warned 'em."

"What are they doing here?" asked Elly, holding the scruff of Bear, keeping him close beside her.

"Prob'ly after the same outlaws we are, I heard Bear Face, or Hickam, tell White Skunk they'd get the gold and buy 'em some rifles, and these boys are prob'ly wanting those same rifles."

"Can we stop 'em?" asked Elly, frowning and looking back to where the two scouts had disappeared into the timber.

"Do you wanna get between three outlaws and more than a dozen renegade Indians?"

"Uh, no, but aren't we supposed to take the outlaws into custody?"

Reuben lowered the binoculars, twisted to his side, shaking his head, and looked at Elly, "There ya go again, gettin' all particular and such. Expectin' us to do our job and gettin' us in a fix again!" He grinned as Elly lifted her eyebrows in surprise, and both started chuckling.

A rattle of stones caught her attention and she looked below at the trail to see the two scouts. She touched Reuben's arm, "The scouts, they're returning!" she spoke just barely above a whisper even though the riders were more than a hundred yards below them and moving through timber and across slide-rock making enough noise to mask their words even if spoken aloud.

Reuben turned back to look at the war party, watched as the scouts reported, gesturing up canyon, and turned to lead the way back into the timber to push into the canyon and past the rockslide. A few of the men had rifles, but most were armed with bows and arrows, lances, and all carried their shields either hanging beside their riggings or loosely worn on an arm. As they entered the trees, Reuben counted thirteen warriors, moving single file on the narrow game trail.

"Even if we wanted to, we couldn't reach the outlaws before them," stated Reuben, nodding toward the war party.

"But maybe we can prevent a slaughter," suggested Elly, looking at Reuben with an expectant, perhaps hopeful, expression.

Reuben frowned, "All of these, Ute and white men alike, were a part of the attack on the Schmidts. They're the ones, including the leader of the outlaws, that butchered that family! None of 'em deserve a chance to take another breath!" growled Reuben.

Elly looked at her man, dropped her eyes and quietly responded, "Vengeance is mine. I will repay, saith the Lord."

Reuben exhaled as he slowly shook his head, looking at Elly. "Sometimes..." he started but ended with a shrug and stood. They walked back to the horses and pack mule, tightened the girths, and mounted up. "The only trail further up is on the north side of the draw, and we'll be right on the heels of that war party, so keep Bear close by. Near as I could tell, the camp of those gold hunters was around the big bend yonder, but I dunno how far, so we'll stop and let me take a gander."

"I'm followin' you, just don't get too far ahead of me!" warned Elly, chuckling. She had already declared her intentions about not getting left behind again, and she gave Reuben a sly look of warning even as she smiled.

Just shy of a mile upstream from the rockslide, the canyon pushed back at the hills on the north side, the steep mountain and talus slopes on the south side refusing to give way. Reuben reined up, motioned to the trees on the shoulder to the right and pushed Blue up the bank and into the ponderosa thicket. He stepped down and with binoculars hanging from his shoulder, and the Sharps rifle in hand, he started his climb to the crest of the shoulder.

The hillside was littered with deadfall trees, probably from an old fire or even a stormy blowdown, it made the climb more difficult as he had to move around, climb over, and even crawl under the grey trunks that mingled with new growth aspen, scrub oak, and skinny saplings of spruce and fir. Where the draw widened, the creek bottom blossomed into a collection of beaver ponds, as the stream meandered through the thickets of willows and berry bushes. As he bellied down at the crest of the shoulder, he spotted the war party just entering the trees at the mouth of a dry creek that merged with the little creek below. A thin column of smoke spiraled up from the black timber and as Reuben focused in on the trees, he recognized the roof of an old cabin. It was tucked into the trees and had probably been built decades ago by some trappers in this beaver-rich land.

The war party stopped at the edge of the trees and the leader motioned to his men, moving them apart and into the trees. As the warriors tethered their animals and disappeared into the woods, leaving one of the young warriors with the horses, Reuben watched, recognizing what they were doing, and even though he did not like the idea, he knew he could not just sit back and let the men be slaughtered. He lifted his Sharps, took his aim at the big white trunk of an aspen that had been used to tether a couple of the warriors' mounts and stood about seven hundred yards away, and squeezed off his shot. The big rifle boomed, the blast echoing across the narrow valley, and the bullet buried itself in the thick trunk. The impact startled the two horses that jerked back away from the tree, breaking their ties, and taking off at a run through the trees and back down the trail. Other horses were skittish, but the young warrior settled them down even as he searched the distant trees for the shooter. Reuben turned away and moved as quickly as he could to return to Elly and the horses. He reached for Blue's rein as he swung aboard, "Looks like the outlaws found themselves a cabin, but the war party is spreadin' out and getting ready to attack. That shot'll warn 'em, confuse the war party, and give us a chance to maybe make a difference."

"WHAT WAS THAT?!" BARKED PORK, LOOKING TO THE DOOR and window of the cabin. He looked back at Hickam who came off the bunk and chair, hastening to the window. Freckles had gone upstream of the little creek, hunting for meat that was badly needed. They had neglected their supply after finding the gold but now their bodies were demanding more.

Hickam opened the door a crack, looked to the trees and saw nothing. "That was a rifle shot, but it was down the canyon a ways, don't think it was near here."

"Mebbe it was Freckles, takin' a deer or sumpin'. But what if it was Injuns?!" asked Pork, looking to Hickam, wide-eyed and afraid.

"Then we'll fight 'em!" growled Hickam. "Get yore rifle!"

The cabin had seen better days and that was some time ago. The roof was spotty at best, the chinking between the logs was nonexistent, and the shutters on the windows had been used for firewood, evidenced by the leather hinges that sat on the hearth beside the grey coals. The front of the cabin had one window and the door sported a cross shaped firing port. Another window was on one side, but the other two walls had neither window nor door. Hickam growled, "You take that window!" nodding to the window beside the door.

Both men were quickly in position, rifle barrels resting on windowsills and in the firing port of the door. Hickam stood behind the door, trying to see through the port and cracks of the plank door, while Pork knelt below the window, barely peering over the sill, searching the trees for movement. Listening for any giveaway as to who might be attacking the cabin. Hickam growled, "You're prob'ly right, just Freckles shootin' a deer or sumpin'."

"That didn't sound like his Spencer, bigger, mebbe a Sharps or sumpin'."

"Freckles didn't have no Sharps!"

"That's what bothers me. That marshal had a Sharps."

"The marshal? Couldn't be—White Skunk and the Injuns had him. He's prob'ly dead an' gone by now. 'Sides, what would he be up here for and what would he be shootin' at?"

"Mebbe he shot Freckles," whimpered Pork.

24 / REVENGE

The boom from the rifle startled the warriors who were bent on sneaking through the trees to take the white men by surprise. Those nearest the targeted tree, turned, searching the trees for any sign of another that was behind them, but there were no other shots, no sign of another man, but Big Thunder motioned the men to keep moving toward the cabin as he grabbed one of the nearby warriors, Red Horse, and sent him back to the horses to look for the shooter. He moved slowly, carefully, his rifle held across his chest, wary of the shooter who must be one of the three men they were after. Maybe one man had gone into the valley to hunt for meat and had not seen the war party. He moved at a crouch, flitting from tree to tree, until he came to the edge of the thick pines, and stopped to survey the open valley.

He saw movement downstream, but whatever it was, it was too far for him to make out. He frowned, shaded his eyes against the eastern sun that stood high in the sky and the bright reflections in the water, saw what he thought was some elk, maybe three, moving below the beaver ponds and into the trees on the south side of the valley. He shook his head, looking directly below at the creek bottom, moved away from the trees so he could see around the point and upstream, but still there was nothing. He looked back at what he thought were elk, but they had gone into the trees.

As Reuben and Elly moved into the black timber, he gave Blue his head, letting him pick his footing on the steep slope and work through the trees, using the carpet of needles to silence the footsteps. Reuben leaned to the side, twisting to see through the trees and held up his hand to stop Elly. He stepped down, Sharps in hand, but motioned to Elly to join him as they picketed the horses and mule. He stepped around a big spruce, dropped to one knee, and lifted the binoculars to look toward the cabin. He picked out several of the renegades as they slowly made their approach, unsuspecting of anyone behind them that watched.

"They're moving on the cabin, but nothing has happened yet." Reuben looked around, picking firing positions, still uncertain of what might happen, but he wanted high ground, good cover for both him and Elly. He looked at Elly, "There's nine renegades, one is out near the point," motioning to the timbered end of the ridge that fell from the high peak. "Maybe he was looking for the horses that spooked, or maybe trying to find the shooter that scared 'em." He chuckled, and added, "The others are scattered in the trees below the cabin. It's a bit far for your Henry, so..." he shrugged as he handed her the binoculars and lifted the Sharps, using his knee for support. The scope afforded him a good view as he searched the trees for a target but chose to hold his fire until the war party made a move.

"Ho! Bear Face! I am Big Thunder! I am the war leader; White Skunk was killed. Where are the rifles you promised?"

Hickam looked at Pork, shook his head and faced the firing port of the door and answered, "White Skunk is dead? Who killed him?"

"The woman of the white man we captured! She brought the soldiers to the village and killed him to make Cuchutikay release her man! Where are the weapons you promised?"

"I don't have them yet! We need the gold, and the mountain came down on us before we got the gold. We can't get rifles without the gold!"

"We will take your rifles—you buy more!"

"We can't do that! We need our weapons!"

Big Thunder answered with a blast of his rifle, the signal to the others to start the attack. Two warriors fired their rifles, prompting return fire from the men in the cabin. Other warriors screamed their war cries, moving closer and using their bows, launching a barrage of arrows at the windows of the structure. The rattle of gunfire told Reuben the fight was on, and he picked his target, a warrior starting for the right side of the cabin. He narrowed his sight picture, steadied his rifle, and squeezed off the shot. It was an easy shot for the experienced sharpshooter, no more than four hundred yards and as the smoke cleared from the muzzle, he saw the downed warrior. He scanned the trees, searching for another target. He knew the attackers did not realize they had a shooter behind them, the rattling gunfire of their close-in fighting masking any sound that came from the distant trees, but when another warrior took a bullet in the side under his lifted arm that held a lance, two of the nearby warriors searched the trees behind them, shouted a warning to the others, but seeing nothing, continued their attack.

The side window offered Pork few targets, but he sent some lead into the melee for good measure but did not see any attackers fall. He was well-practiced at reloading the Springfield, using the paper cartridges with a minie ball, and kept up a steady fire, about three shots per minute. But like many a man that is frightened in battle, he thought the more often he shot the better and did little more than bury lead in the tree trunks. While Hickam chose his targets and put his single-shot muzzle-loading Springfield to good use, scoring a hit almost with each shot, downing two of the attackers.

The first onslaught was quickly repelled as Big Thunder called his men back. Hickam and Pork reloaded their Springfields, using the paper cartridges with the minie ball and Hickam checked the loads of his Colt Dragoon revolver ensuring the caps were secure and he checked the spare cylinder he carried in his possibles bag.

"Here they come!" shouted Pork lifting his Springfield and firing in the general direction of the attackers, but he had only a glimpse of one warrior. Quickly reloading, he kept his eye on the trees, watching for any target and fired again, just in case there were others, but it did nothing more than add to the smoke at the window opening.

"What're you shootin' at?" growled Hickam. "Wait'll you can see 'em, you idjit!"

"Hey! They're comin' with fire!" shouted Pork, drawing a bead on a furtive figure that ducked behind a big ponderosa, the torch he carried showing past the trunk. He narrowed his sight on the torch and squeezed off his shot, blasting the torch into bits. But the pieces of the torch dropped into the thick bed of long needles and quickly began to flare up. "The fire's startin' at that tree! It'll spread to the whole forest! We gotta get outta here!" screamed Pork, looking back at Hickam, wide-eyed and jittery.

"Just keep 'em away from the cabin!" shouted Hickam, squeezing off another shot through the firing port of the door. He heard the impact of the bullet as it struck the side of an attacker that thought he was behind the cover of the tree, but Hickam had marked the side of the man for his bullet and sent the messenger of death, but unknown to Hickam, it plowed a furrow through the muscle at the man's back. The Indian slumped to the ground, kicked his leg once and lay still. "That's three!" muttered Hickam as he tore the paper cartridge with his teeth, readying his load for the rifle.

Hickam dropped the Springfield, dragged his Spencer from under the bed and grabbed the pouch of Freckles's with the cartridges. He fumbled with the magazine assembly, and fought to load the unfamiliar weapon. Although he had the rifle for some time, his preferred weapon was the Springfield, but now he needed more firepower and knew the repeater Spencer could put out two to three times the number of bullets as the Springfield. Fear was getting a grip on the big man. Never before did he ever think he was anything but invincible, but he had seen the furtive Ute warriors and knew they were greatly outnumbered. He lifted his Spencer, pointed it in the general direction of the attack and fired, jacked another round, closed the breech, cocked the hammer, and fired again, repeating the action until his magazine was emptied. He lowered the rifle, pulled out the magazine assembly and began stuffing cartridges into the tube, filling the magazine with another seven cartridges, he slapped the spring assembly into the tube, snapped the butt plate closed and lifted the rifle to the window. He moved to the window, motioning Pork to the side window, rose up to look, the barrel of the rifle extending from the windowsill, but was shocked when a hand grasped the barrel and jerked the rifle from his grip. A warrior screamed, stood with raised lance, and sought to drive it into the chest of the shocked Hickam.

The big man knocked the lance aside, fell back, and grabbing the shaft of the lance, jerked it from the warrior. He stumbled back, tossed the lance aside and grabbed his Springfield. He stepped to the window, bringing the rifle to full cock and dropped the hammer, his sight on the back of the fleeing man that carried his Spencer, but just as the rifle roared, the warrior moved behind a big spruce. Hickam growled and shouted, dropped his rifle down to reload as Pork turned, saw his friend fumbling with the muzzleloader, and saw another warrior charging the window. He lifted his rifle and fired, saw blood blossom on the Indian's shoulder as he stumbled forward and fell with his captured rifle beneath his bloody body.

"Check that side window! Hurry!" shouted Hickam, unconcerned about the fallen warrior, focused on his reloading. "We gotta get outta here!"

In the instant that Hickam had turned to look at Pork, a torch landed at the door and smoke lifted to obscure the firing port. He kicked at the door, trying to push the torch away, but the dried and weathered wood of the door had already caught fire and flames flared up, obscuring his view, and hindering their escape. Hickam turned to look at the window, peered around the edge, looking to the trees, searching for any attackers. All he saw was the flames from the fire at the foot of the ponderosa and the splattered torch hit by Pork. The tall tree flared, the dry cluster of needles on each branch acting as individual torches and turning the towering tree into an inferno, flames licking at nearby trees and spreading. The heat from the fire moved rapidly on the uplifting breeze.

Pork fired from the window at a running figure that carried a torch, he scored a hit and the man stumbled, dropped the torch, and fell on his face, but before Pork could reload, the warrior came to his feet, looked back at the cabin and took cover in the trees. Pork lowered his rifle, beginning his reloading, but watching the trees for any other attackers. He went through the motions of loading by rote, tearing open the cartridge, dropping the powder down the muzzle, ramming home the paper and minie ball, placing the cap on the nipple and readying his shot. As he lifted his rifle, Hickam hollered, "Here! Help me get out this window! We gotta get outta here!"

Pork turned away from the window, went to Hickam and with a glance out the window, he dropped to his knee and put a shoulder under the rump of the big man. "Easy, easy, muh leg's still broke!" whined the big man as he put both hands on the windowsill and bellied over, rolling out and onto the ground. He struggled to his feet, leaning against the side of the cabin. He turned to the window, "Hand me muh rifle!"

Pork pushed the long muzzleloader Springfield through the window, leaned out and looked around. He had a sling on his rifle and slipped it over his head and shoulder, grabbed the sill board and lifted himself as he toed the edges of the logs beneath. He bellied over, looked up, and caught an arrow at the base of his throat. He choked, grabbed at the shaft, and fell out onto the ground, driving the shaft of the arrow through his throat to protrude from the back of his neck. Hickam stared at the figure of his friend at his feet, looked up to see three warriors approaching, the most prominent being Big Thunder. The war leader glared at the big man, "Bear Face!" he growled as he lifted his big war club high, but the bullet from Hickam's rifle shattered his hair pipe bone breastplate, split his sternum, and blasted out the man's back, taking part of his spine with the slug. Big Thunder appeared to melt where he stood, dropping the war club from lifeless hands, and falling in a heap. The two warriors beside him, Red Horse and Creeping Bear stopped, looked at their leader, looked at Bear Face as he struggled to reload his rifle, and lifted their weapons. Creeping Bear fired his rifle just as Red Horse loosed an arrow and both projectiles found their mark, blossoming red on the big chest of the defiant Hickam who snatched his pistol from his belt and fired at each of the men, striking Bear in the shoulder and Horse on his hip, but before he could fire again, his legs gave way and he dropped to the ground, his whiskery face falling into the burning needles and smoke wrapping his body in a wispy blanket.

The two warriors looked at one another, checked their wounds and snatched at some moss on the unfired trees, stuffed the moss against the wounds that were nothing more than deep creases, and started from the trees, fleeing the roaring flames.

The fire roared, consuming everything in its path.

Trees snapped and crackled, birds took flight, animals fled, and the stench of burning flesh filled the woods. The wind whipped down from the tall mountain peak, driving the flames before it and pushing the fire to exhaust itself as it was swallowed up in the wetlands of the beaver ponds and greenery that edged the little creek. Smoke lifted in thin spirals; silence covered the valley bottom.

Reuben had seen the young warrior with the horses as he drove the animals from the trees, away from the flames, and gathered them in the muddy flats by the beaver ponds. Now the only movement was that of the fleeing renegades, some appearing to be wounded and clinging to the manes of their mounts, laying low on the necks of their horses as they clattered across the edges of the slide-rock that lay at the foot of the talus slopes.

Reuben and Elly stood and watched the renegades disappear down canyon, shaking their heads as they looked back at the still smoking, fire-scarred hillside and ridge. Reuben looked at Elly, "Guess that's over. We'll let the fire cool off a mite, then go check the cabin. So, how 'bout some coffee?"

Elly chuckled, "You and your coffee!" as she walked to the horses and pack mule to fetch the makings.

25 / REPRISAL

At the first rifle shot, Freckles dropped from his mount and took cover in the trees. In the narrow draw, echoes bounced between the steep-walled mountains, masking the origin of the gunshot. Freckles never considered himself cowardly, just smart. He knew when to hide and when to stay away from trouble and whenever there were gunshots, it was not the safest place to be riding or even hunting. Anyone that knew the lanky man with the carrot top hair, might use many words to describe the man, but brave was not one associated with Freckles. As he stood in the trees, he looked about for a better place to hide, but seeing none, he stood his ground, watching the valley bottom for any sign of trouble. He waited a good spell and was just considering mounting up and moving further up the canyon in his search for game, when more gunfire erupted. He could tell this was from just over that low ridge where the cabin was and where Hickam and Pork were waiting.

He stepped back, turning to look into the deep timber, and grabbed the lead of his mount and started into the thicker trees. He spotted a big, downed spruce, the root ball standing half again higher than his own six plus feet, and led the horse to the far side, tied him off and pushed through the branches to make a cubbyhole to hide. Once settled in, he rolled out his bedroll and stretched out, the distant sporadic gunfire muffled by the thick trees, and with a grin, he put his hands under his head, crossed his ankles, and closed his eyes. He thought, *maybe if I'm lucky, they'll kill 'em both, leave the country, and I can get all the gold!* He smelled smoke, frowned, and chuckled at the thought of his riches and fell asleep.

THE STENCH OF BURNED FLESH ASSAULTED THEIR SENSES, forcing them to cover their faces with their neckerchiefs. The horses had been tethered on the far side of the dry creek bed, and Reuben and Elly plodded through the ashes, moving to the remains of the cabin. A half wall still stood at the back, but the rest of the cabin was nothing but jointed corners and stubs of partially burned logs. As they approached the still smoldering remains, they stopped, seeing the forms of two men, obviously the outlaws as was easily seen by the hobnail soles on the blackened boots. "Looks like the renegades took their weapons, not even a knife blade is left," observed Reuben. "Not enough of them left to try to bury." He paused, looking around, "Peers to be a body yonder, reckon that's a native," he spoke as he walked closer, pushed at the shaft of a war club, saw some bits of hair pipe bone that was part of a breastplate. "I'm thinkin' this was the leader of the bunch, I think his name was Big Thunder."

Elly stood still, her hand at her mouth keeping the

neckerchief in place covering her nose and mouth, as she looked around. She pointed to the tree stubs, "Looks like another body yonder." Reuben looked where she pointed and started to the other side of what had been the cabin. He remembered shooting at a warrior trying to approach the cabin on that side and as he neared, he could tell it was the body of a warrior and knew it was the same man he shot. He dropped his eyes, always sorrowed to see the death of a man that had died at his hand, no matter the circumstances. He saw another body further away, approached close enough to see it was that of a native, and motioned to Elly to go to the horses.

"There's only two white men, the others were natives. That means there's one missing. Near as I could tell, the two were the big man called Hickam, and the other short fat one called Pork. The third man was the tall skinny one, the redhead, remember?"

"Yeah. I think he was called Freckles, wasn't he?"

"Believe so," answered Reuben, frowning and shaking his head. "I didn't see him with the war party, but I wasn't lookin' too close either. He might'a been." He looked around, turned to Elly, "Did it look like the war party had any extra horses?"

"Yeah, they were trailin' some, but they also lost some warriors. Mighta just been the horses of the dead men."

"Ummhmm, or the horses of the outlaws." He frowned, "Mules?"

Elly frowned at him, "Whaddya mean?"

"Did you see any mules?"

"Uh, no, no I didn't!"

"Course that don't mean much, the natives don't much care for mules so they coulda just left 'em, but if they did, maybe we can find 'em." He turned to look back at the cabin, scanning the terrain, searching for a likely place where the horses and mules would have been picketed. He pointed, "There! Behind and below the cabin, just above where the fire burned. Looks like a clearing below the ridge. That's not too far from the water below, might be where they are, or were. Let's take a look."

They took to the trees to avoid the hot spots and ashes of the fire, rode above and behind the cabin and topped out on the ridge to follow it down to the clearing above the creek. As they broke from the trees, it was immediately evident this had been where the horses were picketed. The droppings, cropped grass, and trampled flats showed horses and mules had been kept here for a few days. Reuben went to the lower end, saw a bit of a trail that pointed to the creek bottom and motioned for Elly to follow. Reuben reined up, stepped down and examined the tracks, stood, and pointed, "One horse went thataway," looking upstream, "but looks like he came back, got the other horses and went downstream, and it looks like we just missed him." He stepped back aboard, swung Blue around to face downstream and stood in his stirrups to look to the east, down canyon, but there was nothing.

Reuben dropped into his saddle, leaned forward on the pommel, and looked at Elly, "So, that's the only way outta here, so we best get movin', but..."

"Yeah, but!" answered Elly, "The war party and the last outlaw—and we could run into all of 'em."

"Weren't you the one that said we had to do our job, get the outlaws?"

"But fightin' off a war party wasn't part of that!"

Reuben grinned, sat back, and with a glance over his shoulder. He looked down at Bear, motioned him forward to scout the trail, waved to the free rein pack mule, and started to the trail.

Red Horse and Creeping Bear rode side by side, talking and planning. Their wounds were minor but painful and others were also suffering, but none complained, it was not the way of proven warriors. When they came from the canyon, where the creek bottom widened and the valley opened, they returned to a previous camp about a mile from the mouth of the canyon and downstream from the rockslide. The grove of aspen, thick with the fluttering leaves, climbed the flank of a timbered knoll on the north side of the creek showing pale green amidst the black timber. The flat, broad bank of the little creek held the thickets of aspen, yet also bore grassy flats that offered both cover and comfort for horses and riders.

As the war party entered the grove, Creeping Bear and Red Horse directed the men to prepare their camp and chose two men to scout their back trail and two to scout downstream. The two leaders had talked about the extra shooter that fired the first shot before the attack and was on the hill behind them during their attack on the cabin. They had assumed it was the third man of the group that had ridden with the one called Bear Face, but Red Horse suggested it might have been the marshal and his woman. Both thought it best to be careful with several of the men wounded and needing attention, for if the mystery shooter followed them, they must be prepared.

"Müwa' ni!" barked Red Horse, getting the attention of all the men but especially the one, called, "fix the wounds!" The warrior nodded, turned to the three men that had already handed off their mounts and were seated near one another on two grey trunks of downed aspen. Two men had deep bullet creases, one on the shoulder, the other across his back. One man had taken a bullet that was a through and through in his side, just above his hip bone. Both Red Horse and Creeping Bear also bore wounds but chose to tend to themselves for now.

Müwa' ni was known as a healer, even though he sought to be a warrior. His father, Black Bird, was the shaman of the village and Müwa' ni had studied with him. He readily gathered the plants and herbs, hedge nettle and yarrow, he needed as they were plentiful near the creek, most growing in the presence of the berry bushes. He also gathered some broad-leafed plantain and quickly made poultices for the wounds, using the plantain as the broad bandage that would be covered with patches of buckskin or blanket.

Red Horse stood before the men, "We will rest here. If the scouts bring word of others, we will fight. We must have time for our wounds to heal, but we will only stay two days." He looked to the others, seeing most nod agreement, then turned away and returned to the edge of the trees above the creek bank, where he and Creeping Bear had made their camp. He looked at the other leader, "Müwa' ni will join us soon. The others are tended, and he will have the poultices for our wounds." Red Horse seated himself at the base of an aspen, leaned back and breathed easy for the first time since he was wounded by the white man called Bear Face. He snarled at the memory of the man, looked to Creeping Bear, growling, "We should have taken the scalp of Bear Face!"

"It was better that he burn!" snarled Creeping Bear. "We have his weapon, but it is no better than what we have! We need far-shooting rifles like the marshal and his woman have!"

"We will look for the man and his woman. You can have his rifle. I will take her rifle and her scalp will be on my coup stick!" bragged the disgruntled leader, wincing from his wound and harbored anger.

"First, we will go to the village of the white men, where this creek," nodding to the trickling stream that still showed muddy from the rockslide, "joins the river called the Arkansas. There we will take the rifles for our men, and others will join us! Then we will drive all the whites from our lands!" declared the defiant Creeping Bear.

Red Horse nodded his agreement, looked to see Müwa' ni approach, and stood. With a glance to his fellow leader, he motioned for the medicine man to tend to his wound. He was determined to become the greatest warrior of the Capote Ute people, but first he must heal.

26 / CAPTURE

The lowering sun was at their backs as they neared the narrowing of the valley. The shoulder of the north mountain pushed into the creek bottom and except for the creek, almost met the bottom of the long talus slope that dropped from the high mountain on the south side. The flank of the north mountain carried a timbered shelf that hung above the little creek and was thick with ponderosa, spruce, and a few aspen. Except for one wide and shallow beaver pond, the creek flowed freely before meeting the bottomed-out rockslide that was holding the water in a deep pool that threatened to break loose at any time. This was where the trail had been covered by the rockslide and forced the travelers to take to the precarious slide-rock.

Reuben reined up above the beaver pond, motioned Elly alongside, and pointed, "We might catch up to the outlaw somewhere along here. If he's smart, he'll be watching the tracks of the war party and keep his distance. It's comin' on dusk, and I'm thinkin' the Indians mighta made camp 'bout where we saw 'em 'fore they came into the canyon."

"That's not much further. Wasn't it just below the mouth of the canyon?" asked Elly, frowning.

"Yup. And I'm thinkin' the only place he can make camp is either on the flank o' the mountain just around this bend, or up on that shoulder where we were before. I figger we'd go back to the same place we were before, and if we catch up to him...well..." he shrugged.

He slipped his Henry from the scabbard beneath the left fender of his saddle, lay it across the pommel, motioned to Bear to stay beside Elly, and nudged Blue forward, taking the narrow bank to the left of the pond. He watched the tracks, recognizing those of the outlaw trailing the mule, wanting to see if and where he left the trail. Reuben drew rein, leaned down to look at the tracks, sat up, and looked back to Elly. He motioned to the tracks, and to the trees on the shelf below the flank of the mountain. Thick pines and a small cluster of aspen offered ample cover for an ambush or a camp. Reuben slid to the ground, rifle in hand, and walked back beside Elly. He whispered, "I'm goin' into the trees yonder, I think he's made camp there and the horses would give us away."

"What about the war party?"

"They kept going, the tracks show he took to the trees, just his horse and a mule."

She nodded as he passed the reins of his mount to her and started to the trees.

His training and experience as a Sharpshooter served him well as he moved through the trees, carefully picking each step, making less noise than the late afternoon breeze that whispered past. The timbered shelf was about five hundred yards along the creek and no more than a hundred yards wide, the trees were crowded but not thick and that forced Reuben to flit from one tree to another, usually moving in a crouch. The shelf was in the bottom of the long gorge and the sun was dropping beyond the mountains, dusk bringing long shadows. Reuben spotted the lone man, gathering firewood and preparing his cookfire. Reuben shook his head at the foolishness of making a fire this close to the camp of the Ute war party, but this was a man that was not schooled in the ways of the wilderness and like many before him, was ruled by his appetites and comforts.

Reuben moved closer, chose a tall ponderosa for cover, and lifted his rifle. "Stand still!" he growled, speaking just loud enough to be heard, but not to give warning to any others within earshot.

Freckles had dropped to his knees to build his fire and at the command, froze in place, looking about but seeing nothing.

"Lift your hands high and don't move!" came another command.

Freckles complied, looking across the fire ring to his rifle that leaned against a log. He wondered if the intruder could see the rifle but chose to wait for the opportunity to dive for the rifle and cover. Suddenly the voice was directly behind him, "Building a fire is not the smartest thing you could do, what with the Ute war party just a little ways down the canyon."

"The Ute? Why, they're friends of mine! I ain't got no worries 'bout them."

"Just like they were friends with your two partners?"

"Yeah, yeah. We was tradin' with 'em, even camped with 'em a time or two."

"With friends like that, who needs enemies?" chuckled Reuben.

"Whatchu mean?" whimpered Freckles, starting to

lower his hands and turn, but was stopped when the muzzle of a rifle was jammed into his back.

"Stand up, but be slow about it."

"I don't understand. Who're you and what do you want with me?" replied Freckles, rocking back on his heels to stand.

"Turn around—slow!"

Freckles slowly turned, recognized the marshal, and dropped his head, "You!"

"Ummhmm, me. Now, we're getting' your horse and mule and you're coming with us." Reuben stepped back, motioned with the barrel of his rifle for Freckles to move to the horses. As he neared, Reuben ordered, "Now, saddle up, put the packs on the mule, and we'll get outta here 'fore the Ute decide to make us join your friends."

"What'chu mean?" whined Freckles, looking back to Reuben with a frown painting his face.

"Since you ran out on your partners, I figgered you already knew. The Ute killed 'em and baked 'em!"

Freckles frowned, shaking his head, and busied himself with rigging the animals. He finished, turned to Reuben, "Look, we don't hafta do this. I can get you some gold, lots of it! It's real close, but we might hafta work at it a little, but it'll make you rich!"

Reuben chuckled, shook his head, motioned to the animals with his rifle, "Get 'em, and come with me." He watched as Freckles turned, took the reins of his horse and the lead of the mule, and turned back to Reuben.

They were met by Elly, leading her horse and the mule into the trees. She motioned them to stop and be quiet. She came close and whispered, "Two scouts! They stopped before they got to our tracks, went after a couple deer by the creek. Reckon they were more hungry than concerned about us or others. If they take a deer and return to their camp, they won't see our sign, but..."

"Where?"

Elly looked about, pointed toward the creek, "Bout in there, I think." She nodded toward a point that was about fifty yards below where they took to the trees. She looked back to Freckles and spoke softly to Reuben, "I see you got long, tall, and lonesome!" chuckling as she nodded toward Freckles. Reuben had taken Freckles' weapons, a rifle, a belt pistol, a skinning knife, and stashed them in his bedroll behind the cantle of his saddle. Elly handed Reuben the reins of the horses and started through the trees.

"What're you..." started Reuben, reaching out as if to stop her.

Elly looked back at him with a grin and shushed him, turned, and went through the trees, moving as quietly as Reuben would, and approached a tree that would give cover and allow her to see the two scouts. She dropped to one knee, looked into the narrow draw where the little creek chuckled amidst the willows and berry bushes. The two scouts were hunkered down over the carcass of a mule deer, gutting and skinning their quarry. They spoke softly with one another, busy about their task and apparently anticipating the taste of fresh meat.

Elly relaxed and leaned against the tree, watching and waiting until the two men stripped the carcass of choice cuts of meat, bundled the cuts in the two pieces of hide, and mounted up. They spoke to one another, gesturing upstream, but one man shook his head, laughed, and started downstream, followed by the second warrior, who grumbled his concerns, but followed anyway.

Elly waited until the two were well downstream

before returning to Reuben and his prisoner. "They're gone. Took a deer, cut him up, and went back to their camp. We can make it across and get to our camp if you're ready."

Reuben nodded, motioned for Freckles to mount, and waited until Elly was mounted and had her pistol pointed at the prisoner before he swung aboard Blue. He looked at Freckles, "Now, you can come along peaceful and if you're lucky, end up living a nice long life. Or, you can try to get away, making us have to shoot you and warn the Utes, and then we might all have a considerably shorter life. What'll it be?"

"Such as it is, I kinda like livin' so I'll go along peaceable."

"Good choice!"

27 / CAMP

They moved by the dim light of late dusk; long shadows stretched from the tall mountains casting the valleys into premature darkness. They pushed across the little creek, parting the willows, and making for the thin game trail that zigzagged up the steep, timbered slope. The early rising moon offered its blue tinted glow to light their passage as the three riders and two pack mules moved quietly on the trail that was carpeted by the needles of the ponderosa and the matted leaves of aspen. As Elly led the way into the clearing atop the flat shoulder that lay in the shadow of the towering mountain, she moved to the familiar camp. Within moments, they had a comfortable camp with horses picketed, gear stacked, and bedrolls laid out. It would be a cold camp, and the few leftover biscuits and pemmican was all that was offered.

Reuben and Elly sat together, using a log as a backrest as they ate the cold meal and talked. "So, what're we gonna do about him?" asked Elly, nodding toward Freckles that sat alone enjoying his food.

"You mean now, or later?"

"Both."

"For now, we'll hafta tie him or sumpin' to keep him from runnin' off or jumpin' us. But for later, I think we'll take him back to the settlement in the valley below like we said, let them do justice or what have you. After all, it was them he stole from."

"But what about the war party?" asked Elly, sipping some water from the canteen.

"Yeah. Guess we'll just have to wait 'em out."

"What if they decide to make a raid on the settlement. You said they were after rifles and the outlaws didn't have enough, so…"

Reuben frowned, looked at Elly, and shook his head. "Maybe I'll hafta send you on ahead to warn the villagers."

"You ain't sendin' me anywhere! We go together or we don't go! That last time I told you, never again," she declared, "'sides, we don't even know if they're gonna raid the village," she added, shaking her head. She had clinched her fist and thumped Reuben's leg to emphasize her point as she glared at him with pursed lips and squinted eyes.

Reuben chuckled, grinned, "Yes ma'am, whatever you say ma'am."

They finished their meal, then Reuben went to the edge of the shoulder to look down into the valley and spotted three small fires in the aspen. When he returned to the trees Elly was arranging their bedrolls, "Reckon the war party is just down below in that patch of aspen. They made their camp there, so we'll have to keep an eye out."

"Not me! I'm sleepin' sound tonight!" declared a smiling Elly.

Reuben frowned, looked from her to the outlaw and

chuckled. Elly explained, "I told Bear to keep a watch on him, and there he sits!" Reuben looked back at their prisoner who was lying on his bedroll, his head turned to face Bear and his blanket pulled up over his shoulder. Bear was stretched out no more than an arm's length away, his head lifted, his tongue lolling and at every move of the man, a low growl came from the big black dog, prompting Freckles to pull the blanket just a little higher.

Reuben chuckled, "Think he's gonna get any sleep?"

"Prob'ly not, but *we* will!" giggled Elly, crawling under her blankets.

THE EASTERN MOUNTAINS WERE BLANKETED IN SHADOWS as the morning sky paled into shades of grey and dusty blue. Reuben stood beside the tall ponderosa, field glasses to his eyes as he watched the waking camp of the Ute war party. By line of sight, their camp was just over a thousand yards away, but the binoculars enabled him to pick out individual warriors and their mounts. Each one had picketed their horses near their blankets and were leading them to water. A few had already kindled a bit of a fire to make their morning meal, others were tending their weapons. Nothing showed specific signs of leaving, but there was something in the way they interacted that gave Reuben the impression they were readying for a raid or a battle. Maybe it was the nagging sensation in the back of his mind or the prickly feeling when the hair on his neck stood tall, something told him that trouble was coming, but what?

He made one last scan of the valley and turned away to walk back to the camp. As he came from the trees, he saw Elly moving the coffeepot away from the flames, Bear still watching their prisoner who mumbled and fussed all the while, and he chuckled as he walked to the little fire. Elly had built the hat-sized fire under the wide spreading branches of a big spruce ensuring the smoke would be dissipated, but Reuben was unconcerned since the war party had their own fires going and they were at least three hundred feet higher and any smells would be difficult to distinguish from their own. He dropped to the ground, leaned his rifle against the log, and leaned back with a cup of steaming coffee cradled in his hands as he smiled at his woman. “Mmmm, this is just what I needed!” he nodded to the strips of meat hanging over the flames and dripping their juices into the fire, “That smells good, too!”

Elly sat down with crossed legs before her as she picked up the withes of meat, passed one to Reuben, “So, what’re they doin’?”

“Same as us, havin’ breakfast. But I think they’ll leave today, not sure where to or what they’ll be doin’, but I don’t like it. After failin’ to get weapons from Hickam, and still wantin’ some, the only place thataway to get weapons is the settlement down below.”

Reuben looked at the prisoner, called Bear away from him, motioned for the dog to lie down beside Elly, “Come on over here, Freckles. Elly’s got some meat and coffee for you.”

The lanky man stood, stretched, and sauntered over to join the couple, seating himself arm’s length from Reuben and facing Elly and Bear across the fire. She extended a willow branch with a piece of hot dripping meat to him, then poured a cup of coffee and sat it within reach.

"So, Freckles, what do *you* think that war party will do?"

The man frowned, ripped at a piece of meat with his teeth, and chewed. "How should I know? I don't know nuthin' 'bout them heathen redskins!"

"You said you were friends with 'em," answered Reuben, watching the man's expressions and waiting for an answer.

"Well, you see where that got us!" growled the redhead, wiping at the drippings at the corners of his mouth. He reached for the coffee cup and held it in his cold hands, savoring the heat of the tin cup.

"What was your partners deal with 'em?"

"Just what you know already. He said if he could get the gold, he'd buy rifles and bring 'em back to 'em."

"But he had no intention of doing that, did he?"

"Hah! Hickam'd stab his own mother in the back if he thought he could make money doin' it!" snarled Freckles, sipping the hot coffee. He looked up at Reuben, "So, what're you gonna do with me?"

"I told the people at the settlement I'd bring you and the goods you stole back and let them do what they would."

Freckles frowned, glared at Reuben, "What d'ya think they'll do?"

"Dunno. Since we've got most of the goods you stole, and your partner's dead, they might let you work it off or somthin' like that."

"Work? Why would I need to work?" asked a startled and wide-eyed Freckles.

Reuben chuckled, looked at Elly, "I think he's more afraid of work than he is of those Indians!"

Freckles growled and hid his face behind the coffee cup as he finished his coffee and tossed the dregs aside, looking to Elly for a refill. She laughed, shook her head, and refilled his cup. He looked at Reuben, "So, what are you gonna do 'bout them Injuns?"

"Nothin' as long as they leave folks alone, but I'm thinkin' they're wanting to raid the settlement to get those rifles your partner promised."

Freckles frowned, "You mean they'd do to the settlement what they did to...to...Hickam and Pork?"

"Worse. They'd probably kill 'em all, burn their homes, mutilate the bodies, and steal everything that doesn't burn, and..." he shrugged, lifting his coffee cup, as he looked at Freckles.

"That ain't right! They can't do that! Them folks never done nothin' to them!"

Reuben sipped at his coffee, watching Freckles, and looking to Elly. He shook his head, "But you and your friends put the idea into their head about getting rifles, so now, they're going to do whatever they have to just to get rifles so they can kill more white people and anybody else that gets in their way."

Freckles dropped his eyes, slowly shaking his head, and mumbled, "I never wanted to hurt 'em. They's good people, and them women, well that'd be just wrong."

"Ummhmm," responded Reuben, watching Freckles.

28 / WARNING

The sun had yet to crest the mountains when the war party rode from their camp. Long shadows painted the valley bottom as the warriors lined out along the little creek, heading northwest. Reuben stood watching with his binoculars, knowing the direction the party took would take them to the confluence of the little creek they had followed into the valley and the one known as Poncha Creek. This trail would also intersect with the wagon road from Poncha Pass and would take them to the settlement at the base of the mountains where the valley of the Arkansas opened to the wide flats that stood in the shadows of the Sawatch Range.

He walked back to their camp, "Let's saddle up. They're goin' downstream, and I think they're gonna hit the settlement. We need to beat 'em there, somehow."

"How we gonna do that?" asked Elly, grabbing things together for the panniers and parfleche.

"Maybe cross over to the other valley. We'll have to see as we go."

"There!" declared Reuben, pointing to the draw with so many aspen, "That's where they had their camp, but above it there's a low saddle that'd be the easiest place to cross over. If we push it, I think we can get ahead of 'em, but it'll take some hard ridin'. Are you up to it?" he asked, looking at Elly.

She grinned, "Any place you can go, I can too. Just watch!"

"Then you take the lead! Let Bear scout, I'll bring up the rear and keep Freckles in line!"

Elly nodded, slapped legs to her Appy, and pointed her to the trees. She spotted a game trail that split the aspen and hung on the right side of the east slope. Without hesitation, she dug heels to the spotted horse and started up the matted leaf trail. It was just over a half mile to the crest, and she topped out without slowing and started down the far side, the narrow trail cutting through the sparse pines and bottomed out in the dry gulch called Starvation Creek. She reined up, stepped down and with a glance over her shoulder, started walking and leading the little mare, giving the horse a breather as they continued down the draw.

"Are you sure that's a woman and not an overseer?" asked Freckles as he struggled with the pack mule and keeping his seat on the steep slope to the bottom.

Reuben chuckled, "Just don't get her mad, then you'll wish you'da been with your partners!"

It was about a mile more until the narrow, dry creek bed opened up to the gulch with Poncha Creek. Elly let her mare get a good long drink and stepped aside for the men to water their animals. She looked at Reuben, forced a smile and said, "I think we can make better time now, the trail yonder," nodding across the little stream, "looks to hug the edge of the creek bottom and appears to be a good trail." She looked at her mare, stepped closer, stroked the horse's neck, and spoke softly to her friend. She looked back to Reuben, "Think we oughta pick it up a little?"

Reuben nodded and stepped back aboard Blue, but before he settled into his saddle, Elly had already pushed across the creek and had kicked the Appy up to a canter. He laughed, shook his head, motioned for Freckles to get to moving, and dug heels to his roan. With a glance at the dust of his woman, Reuben let Blue have his head and shouldered the butt of Freckles's bay, slapped the gelding on the rump, and with Freckles leading the pack mule, and Reuben's mule on free rein, they also began to kick up a little dust.

The sudden clap of thunder startled them and prompted Elly to draw rein. She looked straight down gulch, blue sky with puffy clouds was before them, but to her right and seeming to ride the timbered ridge, a heavy dark cloud hung, loosing a curtain of rain that moved along the same ridge. Reuben pulled alongside, looked at the rain, felt a few drops, "Maybe that'll slow the war party, it seems to be more on top and on the other side. Let's keep moving and maybe we'll get ahead of 'em!"

Elly nodded, slapped legs to the Appy, and took off at a good canter. The draw they followed was about two miles long before it opened wider, and ahead, less than a half mile, the two creeks merged. If they were to meet up with the war party, this is where it would happen. Elly slowed, stood in her stirrups to look down the draw, turned and looked back at Reuben, saw him nod and motion to keep going. She dropped into her saddle and kicked the Appy back up to a canter and lay low on her mare's neck, hoping they would beat the war party to the confluence. Without slowing, she let the mare have her head and the sure-footed mountain-bred mare stretched out and began to run. The half mile was covered in moments and a quick glance up the adjoining draw showed nothing but the curtain of rain, and Elly kept the pace for another hundred yards and slowed the little horse down to a canter, then a walk.

The creek widened and made a horseshoe bend that brought it beside the trail and Elly reined up, stepped down and let the mare crop a little grass and get a good long drink. The others joined her, the horses and mules with sides heaving, the men shaking their heads and laughing, as Reuben said, "For a while there, I thought you'd try to run all the way to the settlement!"

Elly dropped to the ground, leaned back, and stretched out her legs as she looked at Reuben, chuckled with laughing eyes, and answered, "I think Daisy there," nodding to her Appaloosa, "was just enjoying stretching it out. She loves to run!"

The rain clouds were sliding down the mountains and the long curtain of water began to splash on the beaver ponds and creek. The three quickly mounted and started back on the trail, moving at a quick walk, occasionally picking it up to a trot, then a canter, and back to a walk. A little over two miles brought them to the wagon road of Poncha Pass and they kept up the pace, knowing there was about another five or six miles to go to the settlement.

The first cabin was that of the Burnett's. John Burnett and Nat Rich were busy at building an addition to the shed that was used to store the trade goods and the addition would be the trading post. When they heard the sounds of approaching horses, the men grabbed up their rifles, but recognizing Reuben and Elly, they smiled and

John hollered, "Well, hello! You're just in time to help us build!"

"Might need to put the building on hold for a while. You're fixin' to have some unfriendly visitors!" declared Reuben. He leaned forward on his pommel, hands crossed on the saddle horn and added, "There's a war party of Ute renegades not too far behind us." He paused, looked at Nat Rich, "Could you go warn the others, maybe have 'em meet together somewhere that's easily defended?"

John looked at Nat, "Here Nat, bring 'em here. This is the first place they'll see, and we can use both cabins!"

"Yeah!" answered Nat as he ran to his horse that was tethered in the shade of a cottonwood grove. He tightened the girth, swung aboard, and was gone.

John looked at Reuben, "Say, isn't that...?" nodding to Freckles.

"Yeah, he's one of 'em and we got most of your goods on that mule, which is also yours. The other'n was killed by this war party." He turned to Elly, "How 'bout gettin' Minerva ready, and we'll send a couple others in there with you. We'll set up a breastwork of some kind."

He swung down, looked at Freckles, "You can help us, or we can tie you up somewhere, what's it gonna be?"

"I'll help! You've got my rifle, but I've got lots of ammo."

"Then get down, take the horses and mule to the corral yonder, strip 'em, and let 'em loose." Reuben looked at John, "I think it'd be best if we set up along the bank of the little river yonder. They have to cross it and that'd make 'em vulnerable. We can make a breastwork of the brush and rocks and such, but we've got to hurry. They'll be here soon!"

Within moments, Nat Rich brought the other men,

sending the women to join the others in the Burnett cabin. Reuben looked at the others, saw a new face and said, "You look familiar, don't I know you?"

The man grinned, "Yeah, I'm Levi Whitcomb. I was one of the men with the freight wagons that you helped back up in the valley. When we came through here, I decided to stay and make a home. Gonna send for my family, too!"

"Good for you." He looked at the others, explained the plan of building a breastwork on the riverbank and making their defense there. If necessary, they would fall back to the cabins. The six men and Reuben and Freckles set to work and within moments had an adequate breastwork the length of the riverbank at the shallow crossing. It spanned about a hundred feet between stands of cottonwood, and the men picked their positions about ten feet apart and readied themselves for the fight. They had just settled in, some still adjusting their cover, when the word was passed, "Here they come!"

29 / RAID

The mouth of the long valley opened with a finger of land pushing into the broad flats that held the village. Thick cottonwoods trailed the juniper and piñon from the slopes of the long ridge that paralleled the little river, and cottonwoods, alder, and willows masked the far bank, giving way only to the wagon road that followed the creek from the pass. The breastwork fashioned by the settlers was nothing more that branches, rocks, and driftwood dragged from the river. The firing line was about six feet back from the water, the shallow crossing stretched before them. On the far bank and to the left of the road, the trees were plentiful, to the right they were widely scattered, and the undergrowth of scrub oak and berry bushes offered little cover.

Several of the villagers had Henry repeaters, two had Spencer repeaters, John Burnett had a Colt revolver shotgun as well as a Henry. At first sight of the war party when they were on the roadway, the men hunkered down, the rattle of hammers cocking cut through the brush, and Reuben passed the word, "Wait till they hit the water!" But in that instant, the Indians took to the trees and disappeared. Reuben shouted, "Watch the flanks—pick your shots!"

MINERVA BURNETT PUSHED THE DOOR OPEN TO GREET Elly, "Well, Elly Mae, it is good to see you. We didn't expect you to return so soon!"

"Mornin' Minerva," began Elly as he motioned Minerva into the house. "We have things to do!"

Minerva frowned, looked out at the men conferring in the yard by the stack of lumber and back to Elly. "What is it?" she asked, turning as she closed the door.

Elly paused yet believing it best for the truth to be known, after all she would know in a short while anyway, she began to explain, "There's a Ute war party coming!"

Minerva put her hand to her mouth as her eyes flared wide, then immediately began closing the shutters on the windows, "What about the others?"

"They're on their way here. We women will stay in the cabin, and the men will make their fight outside." Elly looked around the big room, "Do you have any weapons in here?"

Minerva moved to the side window, nodded, and pointed over the door, "There!" Elly looked up to see a Springfield muzzleloader that had probably been used by Minerva's husband in the war. Elly shook her head, "Is that it?"

"That's all that's in the house, John has his rifle with him." She turned to face Elly, frowned, "But, there's other rifles, for the trading post, in the shed!" motioning to the yard where the men had been working.

"Is it open?" asked Elly, starting to the door.

"Yes, yes, it is," replied Minerva.

"You make ready for the other women; I'll get some more rifles!" declared Elly, pushing open the door. She saw several of the villagers running toward them, saw the men carrying rifles and moving toward the others in the yard, while the women hustled toward the cabin. Elly recognized Ethel Hutchinson and motioned for her to come with her to the shed. Elly pulled open the door, stepped into the shed, and looked for the rifles. Spotting a stack of rifles standing in the corner, she picked through them for the best of the lot, two Henrys, two Spencers, and one double-barreled Coach gun.

"What can I do?" asked Ethel as she stood in the doorway, watching Elly.

Elly turned, handing the woman the two Henrys, and said, "Take these inside!"

Elly looked for the ammunition, saw the boxes, pried them open and filled her pockets with cartridges and shotgun shells. With the two Spencers and the coach gun in her arms, she stepped outside, kicked the door closed and went to the door of the cabin. Ethel opened it wide, took the coach gun and lay it with the other weapons on the table. Elly dropped the others on the table and began emptying her pockets. She looked at the women who stood watching, expectant and fearful looks on their faces, and Elly chuckled, "Ladies, this is nothing new to you. You know what to do. Now, any of you know how to use these rifles?" she asked, holding up one of the Henrys.

The women seemed to answer at once, some claiming the Henrys, others taking the Spencers, and Ethel claiming the coach gun. Elly looked at Ethel, "You used that before?"

Ethel grinned, "Oh yes, I know it's an up-close

weapon, but they won't get any closer when I let 'em have it!" she declared, nodding as she grabbed the handful of shotgun shells and began loading the double-barreled weapon.

Elly was pleased to see the other women knowingly loading the rifles and she looked around at the shuttered windows. Each pair of shutters had firing ports and Minerva had moved chairs or stools beside each window. The crossbar had been dropped behind the door and the slides on the firing port in the door had been opened. A tall stool stood beside the door. Elly smiled, looked at Minerva, "You have it all set. Good, good." She looked at the other women, "This is not a big war party, maybe ten or so renegade warriors. They were promised rifles by the leader of the men that were here earlier and stole from the Burnetts. Because he told where he would get the rifles, after they killed two of those men, they now want the rifles you hold in your hands. I hope they won't get past the men," she nodded toward the river, "but if they get around them, they'll come here, so how 'bout we show them the business end of these rifles!?"

"Sounds like the proper way to greet 'em!" declared Maribel Rich, rubbing a hand over her swollen belly, but smiling at the others. Elly frowned, remembering her promise to Maribel to help with the delivery of her first baby, and hoped that would still be possible.

Reuben had purposely chosen the left flank position, nearest the thicker woods. Most of these men had fought in the war and were accustomed to the full-frontal attacks and had prepared accordingly, but

Reuben had been a sharpshooter and had spent his time in uniform using guerrilla and sniper tactics and thought the renegade Ute might do much the same. When the war party disappeared into the trees, Reuben focused his attention on the thickets to the left of the crossing, and slowly stepped away from his position, motioning to Joe Hutchinson to move closer to the left and watch.

The shallow river was no more than thirty-five feet wide and showed clear water with a gravelly bottom in most places. Bending back on itself just downstream from the crossing, the thick trees offered excellent cover for the attackers and Reuben moved silently and kept to the cover as he went into the trees. He spotted the first warrior moving behind a big cottonwood, looking about, readying to take to the water. Reuben dropped to one knee beside a burr oak, leaning against the rough-barked tree as he lifted his Henry. With an eye on the break in the willows on the far bank, he narrowed his sight, saw the willows move and the warrior slip into the water. The Henry bucked, the shot rattling through the thickets and across the water, the bullet shattering the collarbone and tearing through the warrior's shoulder, knocking him to his back in a splashing struggle. Reuben jacked another round, searching the trees for another target but nothing moved, until he saw a sapling move, then another. Someone was moving low, trying to get further to his left. Reuben watched, saw the figure rise and Reuben dropped the hammer. The rifle bucked back against his shoulder, and the figure twisted to the side and dropped out of sight. Reuben knew he hit his target but did not know if it was a killing shot. He waited, but nothing moved.

The first shot from Reuben startled the other men, but they quickly looked to the trees, and the flitting image in buckskin drew fire from two or three of the men. War cries and screams came from the far bank and warriors plunged into the water, drawing fire from the men, but only six or seven warriors showed, two were fired on by several of the men and fell under the barrage. Another warrior screamed as he splashed through the water, reached the bank, and scrambled up the grassy slope only to take the full blast from John Burnett's Colt shotgun. The warrior's face was obliterated, his scream silenced, as he fell back into the water, his body buoyant as it bobbed and floated down the stream.

The men searched for more targets, but nothing moved, silence dropped across the willows like a wet blanket and the men looked at one another, until the staccato of gunfire came from behind them. "The women!" shouted Nat Rich, jumping to his feet and starting at a run to the cabin. Bob Hendricks was close behind, frantic about his wife, Susan. They had only been married for less than two years but had grown up together and come west right after their wedding. Now they had dreams of a home and family, thoughts and images that flashed through Bob's mind as he stumbled and ran to catch up to Nat, fearful of what he would find at the cabin.

"HERE THEY COME!" SHOUTED ELLY, FROM HER PLACE AT the door. The firing port was open and she put the barrel of the Henry through, took a quick aim at a big renegade with a hair pipe bone breastplate and choker, waving his war club high overhead as he screamed his war cry. But it was not the last thing that passed through his throat, the .44 caliber bullet silenced his scream and choked him on his own blood as he staggered and fell, his face in the dirt. Elly jacked another round, heard the other women firing, as gunsmoke began to fill the cabin, but the women were steady and kept the barrage of lead flying across the yard and into the trees.

The cabin seemed to rock back when the thunderous roar of the coach gun erupted, and Ethel Hutchinson said, "That'll learn ya!" as she broke open the action and reloaded. She had fired both barrels and the smoke still rose from the muzzles, but she did not take her eyes off the firing port. The smoke outside the shutters hindered her view, but she stuck the barrel out and looked for another target.

"Look out! Our men are out there!" shouted Maribel when she recognized her husband, Nat, running toward them. One of the warriors had turned to face the two men, lifted his bow with an arrow nocked, and drew back, but Nat Rich fired the Spencer from his hip and the blast of the rifle sent smoke and lead to stop the warrior. The arrow fluttered to the ground as the renegade grabbed at his lower stomach, looked down at the blood, up at the white man that was still charging, and fell to his knees. Bob Hendricks lifted the butt of his rifle and struck the man in the face as he ran past, intent on getting to the cabin. He saw one warrior on his face, another near the trees without a face, and the back of one that was running through the trees, back toward the river, but was gone too soon for Hendricks to get another shot.

The men heard the rustling of horses moving through the trees, heard the clatter of hooves as what sounded like three horses took to the road beyond the little finger of a ridge that poked out of the draw.

Nothing else stirred, and the men spoke softly to one another, "Ya think they're gone?" asked John McPherson.

"Dunno, maybe," answered John Burnett.

"Anybody hurt?" asked McPherson.

"Dunno," answered Burnett as he slowly rose from cover. He walked back along the line, saw McPherson and Joe Hutchinson, both of whom were fine, but when he came to their newest member, Levi Whitcomb, he lay on his back, the feathered fletching of an arrow protruding from his throat, sightless eyes open to the blue sky. He shook his head, called to the others, "Whitcomb's dead." Just beyond Whitcomb, Freckles slowly stood, an arrow fluttering from his shoulder, held tight by his fist as he turned to look at the others.

Reuben pushed through the trees, heard the word from Burnett, and walked close to the man, looked down at Whitcomb, glanced over to Freckles, then up to Burnett, "Anybody else?"

"Dunno, but we better check on the women. They were doin' a lotta shootin'!"

"C'mon, Freckles, we need to get that tended to," declared Reuben as he motioned to the arrow in the lanky man's shoulder and started back to the cabin.

30 / RALLY

The women crowded out of the cabin, anxious to see their men. Several paused as they saw the arrow protruding from Freckles's shoulder, but hastened on to meet their men, relieved to see them unharmed. Minerva looked about, her arm around the waist of her husband, John Burnett, and asked, "What about the new man, Whitcomb?"

John dropped his eyes, "He didn't make it. Caught an arrow in his throat. None of us knew he'd been hit till after it was all over." He shook his head, "We'll get to buryin' him right away, long as we know ever'one else is alright."

"Ethel an' Susan are tending to *that* man," she muttered, the memory of what Freckles and his friend did when they stole their goods, as she motioned toward the new framework of the trade post where the women were standing over the seated Freckles and deciding how best to proceed.

"Maybe you should help 'em. You removed an arrow or two when we were comin' out on the wagon train, remember?"

"Oh, I remember, and I'm sure they can do a fine job. I just remember what those two men about did to you and me, and if I got that close to him, I might push the arrow deeper!" she declared, shaking her head as she looked toward the others. She looked about, forced a smile, and when Elly came near, she said, "So! Since we're all together and we run off those natives, maybe we should have a shindig! You know, have us a dinner and maybe even some dancin' just to let a little steam off and feel better 'bout things! What do you think, Elly?"

"I think that's up to you folks. But if I can help, I surely will!" she declared, putting her hand through the crook of Reuben's elbow and letting a big smile split her face as she looked up at her man.

Maribel Rich, with her husband Nat in tow, came closer, "What's that I hear? A shindig?" She smiled as she looked at the other women.

Louisa McPherson, who still held the Spencer repeater in her arms as she stood beside her husband, chimed in, "I think that's a grand idea! Let's do it!" She looked at her husband, "John, how 'bout you and the men put together some tables and benches with that lumber layin' there for the addition, and we'll get busy putting the meal together." She smiled, and glanced to Bob Hendricks who stood with Joe Hutchinson, "And maybe Bob and Joe could get their fiddle and mouth harp and get tuned up for the dancin'!"

While the women giddily began preparing the feast and more, Reuben gathered several of the men and put two to work digging the grave for Whitcomb, and the others used the pack mules to gather the bodies of the renegades, take them to the flanks of the ridge beyond the river and buried them. He knew it was usually the practice of the native peoples to retrieve any bodies of their warriors and tend to them according to their customs, but these were banished renegades and with so few survivors of the band, no one would be coming to gather the bodies. They did their best to show respect for the dead, but the men of the village were a little resistant when Reuben asked to say a few words from the Scripture, but finally relented after understanding that the reading over one of their own, would be done the following day when everyone could attend.

When they returned, the other men had busied themselves making plank tables and benches, and the women had already begun setting the tables and bringing out the food. It was a fine feast and once the meal was finished, the music began and everyone enjoyed the festivities, but the day had been long and tiresome. As the sun painted the western sky over the tall peaks of the Sawatch Range, and lances of gold pierced the blue of the sky, dusk dropped the curtain of darkness and everyone went to their homes, and Reuben and Elly to their bedrolls in Burnett's new barn.

With their bedrolls atop the hay, it was an exceptionally comfortable bed they made for themselves. Bear was snuggled down with the horses in the stalls below as Reuben and Elly lay side by side, hands under their heads to look at the stars peeking through the door of the hayloft. Reuben asked, "What did the women do with Freckles?"

Elly chuckled, "Oh, so you're just now thinking of your responsibility?"

"Well, we been busy," he pleaded, rolling to his side to look at her.

"They talked with Burnett, agreed to let him sleep in the tack shed and if he's alright in the morning, Burnett said he'd give him that horse, a few supplies, and send him on his way."

Reuben frowned, "That's all?"

"Ummhmm. They said since they got most of their goods back, and he fought alongside of the men, that it wasn't worth worryin' about what to do with an outlaw and it'd be best if he just left. They did say that Freckles said he'd never return to his wicked ways, you know, the same promise that every boy caught with his hand in the cookie jar makes. But he did say he would stay away from villages and Indians, prob'ly go back to the goldfields."

"Ummhmm, yeah, I know exactly where he'll go!"

"Where?"

"Back to that hole where they were digging before it caved in on 'em."

"But that's Ute territory!"

"Yup, but let's not concern ourselves about Freckles. We need to get some sleep if we're headin' back to the fort come morning."

THE LEFTOVER CLOUDS FROM THE RAINSTORM BLACKENED the night, dimming the stars and hiding the moon, but Bear came to his feet, startling the horses that sidestepped and turned to look to the big doors that stood open to the night. The movement of the animals below brought Reuben instantly awake, his hand dropping to his side to grasp the Henry rifle. He moved to the edge of the loft, looked down in the dim light to see Bear standing, head high, one foot lifted and a low growl rumbling in his chest. The dog looked up at Reuben and back to the door. Reuben moved to the open door of the hayloft to look into the corral and to the buildings beyond.

The half-moon peeked from the edge of the dark clouds, offering just enough light to distinguish the shadows below. One moved, staying beside the corral fence, moving in a crouch. The feather in his scalp lock fluttering as he moved silently on moccasined feet. The native lifted his hand to the loop of rawhide that held the gate closed, but the sound of Reuben jacking a cartridge into the chamber of the Henry was loud in the night and the man froze. He looked around, moving only his eyes but saw nothing. He stood unmoving, watching, listening, until Reuben spoke softly in the language of the Ute, "No! Leave now while you still live." The words carried in the still of the night and Reuben knew he had been heard, but the man slowly lowered his hand, turned, and looked about.

Reuben was hidden in the shadows of the darkened door and knew he could not be seen from below and he waited, quiet and unmoving, but watching the would-be horse thief. When the man turned, Reuben could see his face in the moonlight and saw he was a young man, probably the horse-holder in the previous raid and now wanted to earn honors by stealing horses from the very people that had turned away the renegades.

"You are young and will live to be a great warrior, but only if you leave now. To die alone will earn no honors. I have counted coup on you, go now, while you live," spoke Reuben, the words given in a low voice, but easily heard and understood in the still of the night.

"Who is it that speaks from the dark?"

"I am Man with Blue Horse, friend to the Mouache and the brothers of the Mouache."

The young man stood tall, shoulders back, turned

and walked from the clearing toward the river, never looking back. Reuben went down the ladder, stepped to the big door with Bear at his side, and saw the lone figure disappear into the brush and trees near the river. He smiled, nodded, dropped his hand to Bear's scruff, "Good boy, Bear."

He climbed back up the ladder, moved to the bedrolls and lay his rifle at his side as he crawled under the blankets to see a smiling and wide-eyed Elly watching. "Was there only one of 'em?"

"Ummhmm. He was a young one, don't think he was in any of the fights, probably watched the horses. After they lost so many, I think he was wanting to gain some honors and steal some horses, but Bear had other ideas."

"Good for Bear!" chuckled Elly, moving close to Reuben and putting her arm across his chest. Reuben smiled in the night, happy in the moment.

31 / ENCOUNTER

The sun was off their left shoulder, hanging bright in the cloudless sky, as Reuben reached down to shake hands with John Burnett, who said, "That Freckles fella got an early start, and I was glad to see him go. I know you went to a lot of trouble to catch him and get the trade goods back, and we're thankful, but the womenfolk just didn't like the idea of an outlaw hangin' around the village."

Reuben chuckled, "I understand, and it's prob'ly for the best anyway. Maybe he'll keep his word and go to the goldfield and make an honest living, but..." he shrugged, "his kind seldom change."

"We're just glad to be rid of him and his kind," added Minerva Burnett, slipping her hand in the crook of her husband's arm. They stepped back from the big blue roan and the pack mule, looked at Reuben and nodded with a smile and a slight wave goodbye. Reuben looked over to Elly, saw her talking to one of the women and he leaned forward to cross his hands on the saddle horn, grinning at the others and nodding toward his woman.

"Will you be coming back?" asked Maribel Rich, taking Elly's hand in hers as she stood beside the spotted horse.

Elly leaned down, looked at the young woman with the dress stretched tight around her middle. "It looks like you've got some time yet, and hopefully things will work out for us to get back this way come fall. That would give us time to get back to our cabin for the winter. Besides, you've got wonderful friends that would be more than happy to share in that blessed time, so don't you worry about things, alright?"

"I know, but as well-meaning as they are, none of them have tended a pregnancy, and..." she shrugged, looking up at Elly with hopeful eyes.

Elly sat up straight in her saddle, looked down to Maribel and smiled, "We'll see you soon!" and looked to Reuben, who nodded, and nudged Blue to start. They rode from the clearing, turned to wave at the few villagers, and looked back at the crossing of the little river. Blue splashed across the shallow waters, the pack mule close behind and Elly followed, with another glance back to see Maribel waving and returned the wave.

"She sure took a liking to you," observed Reuben as Elly came alongside. The wagon road made it easy to ride side by side and they enjoyed the time of being close as they rode.

"I think it was because we are both younger than the other women. She said one of the women had been pregnant before but lost it, and the other women were, well, not too anxious to have a family. They were more concerned about getting the village settled, natives peaceful, and more people about, maybe a doctor."

Reuben nodded, understanding, "And you?"

"Me?"

"Yeah, what are your thoughts about a family?"

"Uh, I don't think it's a usual practice for deputy marshals to have babies!"

Reuben chuckled, "Then maybe we better get shut of these badges and set about making a home and a family!"

Elly giggled, "I can just see you havin' a baby!"

Reuben turned serious as he reined up and looked down at the side of the road. He pointed, "Look there."

Elly leaned down to see the tracks of one horse that came from the right side. They looked to the side of the road where a trail split the low finger ridge and pointed toward the upper end of the wide valley of the Arkansas. They had already spotted the tracks of the three horses of the natives that fled the fight with the villagers, but this was from the other side. Reuben said, "That's Freckles's horse. Same tracks we followed from the fire."

"Didn't he say he was going to the goldfield?"

"That's what you said he told the others. But the only goldfield he's going to is that hole where he and his friends were digging gold and it caved in on 'em. That's exactly what I thought he'd do, just like I said, greed!"

Elly looked at Reuben, nodded to the tracks of the natives, "You think they'll meet up?"

"I think Freckles is so blinded by greed he won't have a thought about the renegades. He probably thinks they're long gone, but even if not, he thinks he can still get the gold."

"From the looks of those tracks, the renegades are most of a day ahead of him, so, he might be alright," surmised Elly, lifting her eyes to the trail ahead. Bear had been scouting ahead and she could see him sitting in the middle of the trail, waiting for them. She nodded to the dog, "Bear's waitin' so..."

Reuben chuckled, "He does a good job of keeping us out of trouble," and nudged Blue back to his quickstep pace. Elly's spotted mare quickened her pace and the pack mule stayed near as they started into the long gulch of Poncha Creek. A variety of oak, willow, and cottonwoods lined the banks of the creek in the bottom of the gulch, some places the trees and shrubs were so thick the stream was completely hidden. Beyond the creek, piñon and juniper clung to steep slopes, often with roots splitting boulders and hanging tenuously where nothing else could grow. Rocky escarpments protruded from the thick growth of juniper, cedar, and piñon high above their right shoulders. The hillsides standing tall and proud, pushing in on the narrow wagon trail which was more of a pack trail than a roadway for wagons. The sun stood high above the timbered shoulders to their left and their shadows creeped closer and would soon slide under the horses' bellies.

They were approaching the junction with the trail that followed the creek south and the road they followed that would cross Poncha Creek and reach the summit of Poncha Pass. Reuben drew rein, motioned for Elly to stop alongside as he frowned, shaded his eyes to look ahead, and nodded, "Looks like turkey buzzards."

Elly looked at her man and looked upstream at the few buzzards floating on the updraft from the gulch. She knew what her man was thinking, and she had the same thoughts as she slowly shook her head. "With the buzzards there, prob'ly nobody else there, at least not alive."

"Yeah," he muttered as he nudged Blue forward. As they rode closer, it was soon evident what had attracted the carrion eaters. A body of a man, stripped and mutilated, lay spread legged on his back, a raven, two coyotes, some magpies, and two buzzards, busy at the remains. High-topped shoes, red hair, and a discarded hat were enough for Reuben to recognize the remains were those of Freckles, the outlaw turned gold hunter. Nothing else remained, he had been stripped, his horse, weapons, and gear taken, and his body brutally mutilated. Even though the killing had been no more than two or three hours before, the stench was already filling the draw and the carrion eaters had done their best to take their fill, while others waited for their turn.

Elly looked to Reuben, "We're not..." she shook her head, looking at the mess.

"No, not enough left to bury, 'sides, they hafta eat too. I don't think Freckles has anything to say about it, but it seems to be a fitting end."

"What about the renegades? Think we need to worry about them?"

"Won't do any good to worry, but we need to be careful. Let's find us a nice, shady place for noonin', let the horses get some graze and us some coffee," suggested Reuben, reining Blue around to take to the roadway that would lead to the pass summit. A low draw came from the left and Reuben dropped from the roadway and took to the aspen that stood beside a thin trickle of water. He grinned back at Elly, "Look good?"

She smiled and nodded, and they quickly dismounted, loosened the girths on the saddles, dropped the panniers from the packsaddle and let the animals have a drink before picketing them to graze. Elly was already busy with a little fire when she motioned to Reuben to fill the coffeepot from the spring-fed stream, and they were soon enjoying the java and some warmed-over biscuits and strips of meat leftover from the breakfast with the villagers. Bear eagerly accepted tossed tidbits, and the horses were busy at the grass, when the horses' heads came up, the mule's ears stood tall as they looked up the little aspen strewn gulley. Bear rose to stand firm and look a different direction, up the slope behind where Reuben sat.

Elly grabbed for her Henry and looked up gulley, but Reuben slowly stood, his hand at his hip on the butt of his Remington pistol, cocking it as he moved. Something moved in the trees and Elly brought her rifle up, cocking it as she did. She had become accustomed to keeping a round in the chamber but the hammer down, now she readied to shoot as quickly as she spotted the target. A buckskin clad, bare-chested warrior was also lifting a rifle, the muzzle pointed her direction, but Elly dropped the hammer first and her Henry bucked, and blood blossomed on the chest of the warrior, knocking him back as his rifle roared and spat smoke.

Elly quickly jacked another round into the magazine of her rifle, looking at the warrior in the trees. He had crumpled to the ground, but there was still movement. She saw the man twist around, struggling with his rifle trying to bring it to bear, but Elly shook her head, whispered, "Don't do it," and fired. The impact of the bullet that struck the man's face, drove his head back to the side, and the man twisted and dropped to the ground, stilled in death.

As Reuben turned, a war cry screamed through the trees, and he only had a glimpse of a hurtling body flying at him from the trees. He brought up his pistol but was knocked back, the warrior's weight carrying them both to the ground. His pistol was knocked from his hand as he fought with the man who sought to strike with his tomahawk. Reuben knocked the hand with the hawk aside, bringing his elbow back against the man's jaw, driving him away. Reuben scrambled to his feet, but the warrior jumped up and lunged at him again, tomahawk lifted to strike at his head. Reuben ducked under the blow, driving his shoulder into the man's chest, and pushing him back against the big boulder.

Elly had dropped the lever of the Henry to bring another cartridge into the chamber as she slowly turned, looking to the trees for any other attackers. Bear was at her side, looking to the horses, and into the trees, but nothing else moved. The ruckus behind her caused her to look to her man and see the struggle. She moved a little closer, eyes wide, fearful of what might happen but the two were intertwined and she could not risk a shot. She watched, breathless, as the men grappled.

Reuben grabbed at the man's right wrist, drove his knee into the man's groin, and grabbed at his other wrist, but the warrior was too quick and clasped Reuben's arm. The two fighters pushed against one another, grunting and grimacing, neither giving, until Reuben dropped his left shoulder and drove it into the man's throat, forcing him to loosen his grip on Reuben's arm. When his arm was freed, Reuben snatched his knife from the sheath at his back and slashed down, cutting the muscle on the warrior's shoulder, drawing blood and a scream from the fighter.

The warrior pushed against Reuben's chest, but Reuben, still gripping the man's arm with the hawk, drew back his right arm and drove the knife blade to the hilt in the man's gut, twisted it and cutting side to side. Blood flowed, spurted, and covered Reuben's hand, arm, and side. The warrior grimaced, snarled, and spat in Reuben's face, then sucked his last gasp of air, trying to push Reuben away, but Reuben would not give until the man's dead weight began to slide down the blood-covered boulder. Reuben stepped back, releasing his grip on the man's arm, watching him fall. When he stared with sightless eyes to the dirt before his face, Reuben knew the man was dead and turned to look at Elly, relieved to see her standing, unharmed.

32 / REUNION

"I've been thinkin' 'bout those hot springs, are there any on the west edge of the valley?" asked Elly, looking at Reuben with a coy smile as they rode side by side, on the wagon trail toward the crest of Poncha Pass, pack mule following as they led the two horses of the renegades.

"I think so, seems to me there was somethin' said about there bein' an artesian spring of hot water somewhere south of that cone mountain, the one at the mouth of that valley where we saw that other band of Ute. You know, the bunch that hit those freighter wagons," answered Reuben, trying to look stern and unconcerned at the same time.

Elly chuckled, "Now you know you could use a bath even more'n me, we're both gettin' so ripe we can't hardly stand one another!"

"Speak for yourself! I'll have you know that rain th' other day was quite refreshing. Why, I thought I was smellin' as sweet as a patch of columbines!"

"When you wash, be sure to clean your nose cuz your smeller ain't workin' properly!" kidded Elly, laughing at her rumpled man, still showing dried blood on his tunic from his fight with the renegade.

They crested the pass and reined up for a good long look at the far stretching San Luis Valley. With timbered hills that marked the beginning of the rampart of the Sangre De Cristo Range on their left, and the black shoulders of the San Juan Range on the right, the carpet of sage and greasewood mixed with myriad kinds of cacti and grasses that parted the two and marked the way south, the arc of cloudless sky completed the frame of the majesty of the Creator. They took a few moments to bask in the wonder and beauty of the panorama, looked to one another and smiled, both understanding the marvel before them that spoke of a great and mighty God.

With a deep sigh, Reuben nudged the long-legged roan forward, and the couple renewed their travel on the last leg of the journey around the vast San Luis Valley. Elly pushed the little mare to match the pace of the roan and looked at Reuben, "Here's hopin' we can make it all the way back to the fort without any problems."

Reuben grinned, looked at his beautiful partner, and said, "Yup, here's hopin'!"

THE SUN APPEARED TO BE STANDING ON SPINDLY LEGS AS lances of gold radiated from the brilliant orb. The bellies of clouds glowed with oranges and pinks as the Creator put on the last display of light and color for the day. Elly and Reuben stood arm in arm in the shade of the cone-shaped hill that had at one time, eons ago, spouted with a brilliance that rivaled that of which they now enjoyed. Black basaltic rock littered the lower slope of the giant anthill-shaped butte, mute testimony to the forces that lay just beneath the surface of the valley. After riding about fifteen miles into the valley, they had made their camp in the trees between the creek and the rocky shoulder of the cone-shaped butte. It offered ample grass for the animals, and fresh water in the gurgling creek, making for a comfortable camp.

"Well, we didn't make it to the hot springs, but it's not far and it'll feel good in the morning!" declared Elly, her arm around the waist of Reuben as she leaned against his shoulder.

"When I was up on the hill, I could see the steam from the hot springs. I guess it's not but five or six miles from here. We can have our mornin' coffee and such, take our time and get there 'fore the sun's too high."

"I'd like that," answered Elly, hugging him closer.

WHEN THE FIRST LIGHT OF EARLY MORNING PAINTED shadows on the faces of the jagged peaks of the Sangre de Cristo Range, Reuben was atop the butte, spending his time with his Lord and making his visual reconnaissance of the valley. He turned away from the wide-open valley, gathered his gear, rifle, Bible, and binoculars, to start his descent, but was stopped when he saw a group coming from the mouth of the long Kerber Creek valley. He sat down and lifted his binoculars for a better look, recognizing the band to be mostly women, some riding, others walking but most carrying at least one parfleche. As he watched, they spread out through the grassy flats that sided the creek and began looking about, often dropping to their knees, and were gathering some form of greenery. They moved slowly, some with digging sticks, and he soon recognized the women were digging yampa roots. He grinned, gathered his gear, and hastened back to the camp.

He was grinning as he walked into camp, was greeted by Bear and a smiling Elly who poured him a cup of steaming coffee. "So, what are you so cheerful about this morning?" she asked.

"Looks like the women from the Ute camp are gathering yampa roots," he nodded toward the creek and meadow upstream from their camp.

"Oh?" replied Elly. "I guess it would be a good time for that. Maybe I should too!" she declared.

"I'm not too sure how friendly they might be, seein' as how you killed one of their great warriors!" chuckled Reuben, sipping his coffee.

"But didn't you say you talked to a couple of the women about Heaven?"

"I did, but I don't know if they're with that bunch. I s'pose we could go see. I did promise to bring 'em a Bible and maybe teach 'em how to read."

"We could give 'em a Bible, but I think it'll take longer than a day or two for them to learn how to read," said Elly, walking to the stacked gear to fetch a Bible. They always carried at least a couple Bibles, sometimes more, for just such an occasion as this. They seldom passed a store or trading post that they failed to buy any extra Bibles they might have on hand. When she returned to the side of Reuben, she sat on the log beside him and asked, "You wanna come with me, introduce me to the women?"

"Sure, I can do that. We could take along the spare blankets in case we go to the hot springs, too."

Elly smiled at the thought of the hot springs, grabbed a parfleche and asked, "Ridin' or walkin'?"

"Most of them are walkin' so..." shrugged Reuben, making a sling for his Henry to hang from his shoulder. He wanted the rifle handy, but not threatening and preferred to carry it behind his shoulder. He nodded for Elly to lead the way and they pushed through the willows, waded the little creek, and came up on the grassy bank to stand and wait for the women to see them, before approaching.

The women were scattered in the tall grasses, looking for the little flat white blossoms on the tall wiry stem that distinguished the Yampa from the grasses. Reuben guessed there to be about twenty women, all ages and appearances, but away from the creek in the waving grass, he spotted three or four younger women. One of them looked up, saw the couple at the edge of the willows and spoke to the others, motioning toward Reuben and Elly, who stood, watching. The word quickly spread among the women, and they all stopped in place, watching the couple, waiting to see what they would do, until one of the young women spoke to another, and started toward Reuben and Elly. As she neared, Reuben recognized Little Bird, one of the two young women that had tended to his feeding and more, while he was a captive of the Ute village.

He raised his hand to wave and both he and Elly stepped forward to greet Little Bird. She smiled as she neared the couple, "You are Man with Blue Horse, and you are his woman."

Reuben turned to Elly, looked at Little Bird, "Little Bird, this is my wife, Yellow Bird."

Elly stepped forward, smiling, and nodded as she spoke, "Little Bird, my husband told me of you and White Crane. He also said he had promised you a Bible," she held out the Bible toward her, “This is our gift to you.”

Little Bird timidly stepped forward, her eyes never leaving the Bible that was offered. She looked at Elly, down to the Bible and held out her hand to touch it, and as Elly pushed it toward her, Little Bird accepted the book with a broad smile. As she held it with one hand, she slowly and carefully opened the cover, began slowly flipping the pages and paused, then looked to Reuben, “You said this was the Word of God and that He speaks to us, but I do not hear Him.”

Reuben smiled, “We will teach you to read the words on the pages,” he reached for the Bible, opened it to the first book, and began to read, “In the beginning God created the heaven and the earth,” he lifted his eyes to Little Bird who watched with wide eyes, a slow smile splitting her face.

“Will it take a long time for me to learn these words?”

“It will take some time, perhaps you could come to the fort, stay with us and we will teach you.”

“Will you show me the words you spoke when you told us about your God and this Heaven?”

“We will. But now, my wife would like to dig yampa with you, and later we plan to go to the springs to bathe.”

Little Bird smiled, looked at Elly and reached to take her hand. “Come with me, I will help you dig the yampa, and then we will gather some timpsila. Then we will all go to the hot springs and bathe.”

Elly looked at Reuben wide-eyed, “Oh no you don’t! We women will bathe, then you can jump in all by yourself!” Both women giggled as they looked at the expression on Reuben’s face and trotted off together to dig the roots. Reuben turned back, shaking his head and chuckling.

The women finished their harvest of the Yampa, opted to go to the hot springs and harvest the timpsila on the way back. From the cone to the hot springs was about five miles but the women were used to the walk and before long, had finished their bath and were on their way back. Elly, Little Bird, and White Crane came into the camp where Reuben was busy cleaning their weapons. Elly smiled, "I was going to send you to the hot springs, but Little Bird wants you to mark the passages in the Scriptures that you spoke to her about."

Reuben chuckled, "I can do that, if you can stand the way I smell just a little longer."

Elly giggled, looked at Little Bird, "You might have to hold your nose!"

Reuben accepted the Bible, dug in his possibles pouch for the stub of a pencil and opened the Bible as Little Bird sat next to him on the log. He flipped to the first verse, I John 5:13, *These things have I written unto you that believe on the name of the Son of God,* he paused, adding "That's Jesus, the Son of God, remember?" As she nodded and smiled, he continued, *that ye may know that ye have eternal life,* "That's to live in Heaven for all time," *and that ye may believe on the name of the Son of God.*

He continued through the scriptures, giving a brief explanation with each verse. "Remember, four things you need to know, the first is, we're all sinners, *Romans 3:10 and 23,* and the punishment for that sin is death, that's to die and go to the terrible place called Hell. *Romans 5:12 and 6:23a.* But God made a way, so you don't have to go there, and that way is Jesus. He bought the gift of eternal life for you. *Romans 5:8 and 6:23b.* All you have to do is receive that gift. *Romans 10:9-10, 13.* And it also says in *II Corinthians 5:17* that you are a new creation. A brand-new person!"

Little Bird showed a broad smile, glanced to White Crane who nodded and smiled, and looked back to Elly and Reuben. "You have marked these verses, and if I come to the fort, you will teach me to read these?"

"We'll be happy to teach you to read these verses and all the other verses in the Bible," declared a smiling Elly who opened her arms and gave both women warm hugs, smiling and laughing together.

"Well, guess that's my cue to go to the hot springs," mumbled Reuben, going to his roan and mounting up, the extra blanket and change of clothes tied down behind the cantle. He chuckled and waved as he rode from the camp, leaving the three women giggling and talking as they began to prepare some of the new harvest for their meal, as the other women of the village returned to their homes.

33 / RETURN

The women embraced, happy faces all. Reuben grinned as the two young women climbed aboard the two horses that had belonged to the renegades, turned, and took to the trail that sided Kerber Creek and would take them back to their village. Elly gave one last wave, looked up to Reuben and stepped into the stirrup and swung aboard her Appaloosa mare. "I hope they come to the fort. White Crane already helped me with the language of her people, and I would like to teach both of them to read. They're very special young women."

"They are, and it's natives like them that will be the hope of their people in the generations to come," answered Reuben, giving Blue some leg pressure to start them on the trail south.

"Well, aren't *you* quite the philosopher this morning," chuckled Elly, moving alongside.

Reuben grinned, "That's just the way of people. For any people to survive, there must be some that are willing to make whatever changes are necessary, without compromising their values and morals. White Skunk did not want to change, and the evil in the man drove him to put the blame on others and he used that as an excuse to kill. But even that was against the way of his people. Yet Little Bird wanted hope and more and when I helped her understand, she made her choice. I know her people don't often accept women as leaders, but perhaps she will find a way to help her people in the years ahead."

"I hope so. Maybe by her learning to read, that will help her and her people."

"I'm sure it will," answered Reuben. He nodded to the south along the edge of the hills, "It's prob'ly gonna take us most of three, four days, maybe more, to get back to the fort seein' as how we're makin' the big circle and we'll be stayin' near the hills and such."

"Do you think we'll run into any more renegades?"

"Dunno, but there are plenty of natives." He waved his arm toward the San Juans, "That's all the land of the Ute, the Capote, Mouache, Tabeguache, Weminuche. And down south there, that's gettin' into the land of the Jicarilla Apache and the Navajo. So yeah, there's lots of natives, but it's not them that concern me, it's the gold hunters and settlers."

They rode in silence for a while, each with their own thoughts and concerns, but when Reuben drew rein, the motion brought Elly back to the present and she frowned, "What?"

Reuben leaned back, fetching his binoculars from the saddle bags, sat up with glasses in hand and looked to the east across the valley. "Three wagons, maybe settlers, movin' this way."

He watched them a moment, lowered the glasses and looked at Elly as he re-cased the binoculars, "Reckon we better go make their acquaintance."

THE FOOTHILLS OF THE SAN JUANS WERE VEILED IN A haze, standing like shadows in the mist, each rank of hills showing less and less, the nearest hills about four miles off their right shoulder. In the flats, buffalo grass and gramma waved in the morning breeze; to the south, a patch of cottonwoods stood like a lone sentinel at the edge of wetlands that included a shallow lake. They had just crossed a narrow creek that sided an ancient trail that had been used by traders and trappers and crossed the valley from the Sangre de Cristo Mountains, the mountains that now stood as the eastern rampart that framed the San Luis Valley. The wagons had drawn up at the edge of the greenery by the creek and were beginning to make camp as Reuben and Elly approached. Reuben lifted one hand, called out, "Hello, the camp!"

Two men walked from behind a wagon, both holding rifles across their chests as one hailed, "Come on in, if'n yore friendly!"

As they approached, the men at the wagon realized one of the visitors was a woman and he grinned, "Welcome folks. Step down and join us for our noonin'." The man that spoke wore corded britches held up with galluses over a broad expanse of belly that bounced as he chuckled. Thick reddish-gray hair tried to escape his floppy felt hat and join with the full face of whiskers that matched, doing little to hide the red bulb of a nose and laughing eyes that sparkled in the midday sun. "I'm Claude Whipple, and this here's Humphrey, muh brother!" The smaller and younger of the two appeared to be a slightly miniaturized version of his older brother save for the grey in his beard, as his was auburn red. Humphrey added, "Pleased to meet you folks. Join us, please!" he declared, lowering his rifle to set the butt plate on his boot toe.

As they spoke, two women leaned around the corner of the first wagon, both wearing bonnets, looking to see the visitors. When they spotted Elly, both women walked closer and the older woman said, "Well, Claude, why aren't you fetchin' some firewood so we can make a meal fit fer comp'ny?" as she motioned to Elly to join them.

There were three Whipple brothers, Claude, Humphrey, and Hobart. The three families were traveling together and bound for the western slope of Colorado Territory. As they sat together around the little cookfire, Reuben asked, "So you just set out from Amarillo all by yourselves?"

"Oh no, we joined up with a big wagon train, there were seventy-one wagons when we pulled out. But when we got to Santa Fe, five of us decided to take the north branch of the Old Spanish Trail and come into Colorado Territory, the others were talkin' 'bout, well, some of 'em takin' the branch that would take 'em up to Oregon country, the others were dead set on goin' to Californy!" explained Claude.

"You said there were five wagons that came north?" started Reuben.

"Yeah, yeah, th' other two left us this mornin', over yonder by the mountains. They was goin' on north, said they was goin' to the goldfields. But we'ns, well, we're just farmers and we heard tell from an ol' mountain man 'bout the land on the west slope yonder, that it was empty and fertile and good for farmin'." He sat back, thumbs in his galluses, and said, "We'ns prefer to make our own gold in the likes of wheat an' such."

"Have any trouble with the natives?" asked Reuben.

"Nah, we saw some Navajo, leastwise that's what the

wagon master said they was, in Santa Fe, but none since. The wagon master kinda drawed us out a map, showin' this part o' the trail an' it's been good so far. Do you know this country, can you tell us how fer it be to the west slope an' that good farmland they told us 'bout?"

"I don't know how good the land is for farmin' but you're less'n a week from the western slope. There's a pass, Cochetopa Pass, named by the Ute meaning the pass of the buffalo, through the cut yonder, that'll take you through the mountains and put you into the valley of the western slope, some are callin' it Gunnison after a young captain that was killed explorin' the area."

"Kilt? How'd he get kilt?" asked Claude, frowning.

"The Ute, they didn't want white people invading their territory, especially the soldier boys."

Claude shook his head, looked at his two brothers and back to Reuben, "Whatchu think we'ns oughta be doin'?"

Reuben took a deep breath that lifted his shoulders as he looked at each of the men, "Well, the way I see it, you're already here and you're in the middle of Ute country. Whether you keep goin' or turn back won't make much difference. Ahead, you'll be cuttin' through the land of the Capote Ute and they're, well, not too friendly but for right now, they're not out for scalps either. The further you go, you'll be into the land of the Tabeguache, and they are trying to make a peace treaty with the government. Wherever you go, you'll probably run into gold hunters and natives."

Claude looked at his brothers, each one slowly nodded, and looked back to Reuben, "Then I reckon we'll just keep goin'."

"Do you have plenty of weapons and ammo?"

"Uh, we each got us a good rifle, Humphrey also has a

shotgun, we got us a couple pistols. We done alright so far."

"Do your women know how to shoot?"

Claude frowned, "Uh," and glanced to his brothers, "yeah, I reckon. Why?"

"Because where you're going, you're gonna need every rifle loaded and ready and every adult shooting! We've seen enough of what the renegade Indians can do, and you don't want that. Listen, we've got a couple spare rifles we can let you have, and you'd do well to have a weapon by every one that can possibly use one," Reuben nodded toward four youngsters, all less than ten, "and keep them close by."

REUBEN AND ELLY BID THEM GOODBYE, WATCHED AS THE farmers started the lumbering oxen moving, waved, and turned back to the south to make some more miles before dark. The next four days were uneventful, as they moved almost due south until they neared the Rio Grande River, turned east, and rode into the central compound of Fort Garland on the evening of the fourth day. The same officer's quarters were open for them and as they dropped their gear on the stoop, Elly peeked inside, smiled, and turned to look at Reuben, "Almost feels like we're home!"

"Almost, huh?"

"Yeah, how 'bout you talk to the captain, and I'll try to make this feel more like home."

Reuben returned, long-faced and quiet, but forced a smile when Elly met him at the door. She frowned, "What's got you so somber?"

"Ah, Captain Kerber was tellin' me that Kaniache and the Mouache are causin' problems down south and appear to be headed this way. He made a raid down by the Abiquiu Agency because he didn't get the allotment promised, then went to Cimarron and was turned away, so he's on the rampage and no tellin' what might happen. To top it off, Andrew Johnson is now president, and the east is in turmoil what with the war ending and more and more people are comin' west. So, the flood of immigrants and settlers is about to get a whole lot bigger!"

"So, what does that mean for us?"

Reuben dropped his eyes as he stepped through the doorway, following Elly into the main room to be seated at the table. He looked at her, "Well, the way I see it, we can go back to the cabin and hide out and hope the world passes us by, or we can wait 'til we hear from Marshal Holloway or Marshal Moses and see what they have in store for us."

Elly shook her head as she poured Reuben a cup of steaming coffee, sat down beside him, and with her hand on his arm she looked at her man, "How 'bout we just stay here a while, after all, we invited Little Bird to come to the fort so we could teach her to read. And the Tabeguache under Ouray are trying to get the treaty settled and that might bring peace which would solve a lot of the problems, and maybe we can help a little. Now, I'm all for goin' back to the cabin, but it'll still be there whenever we choose to go back. So, let's just wait on the Lord." She smiled and leaned her head on his shoulder. He dropped his head to lean against hers and chuckled, "Yeah, that's always best. Let's just wait on the Lord."

TAKE A LOOK AT: ROCKY MOUNTAIN SAINT

THE COMPLETE CHRISTIAN MOUNTAIN MAN SERIES

Best-selling western author B.N. Rundell takes you on a journey through the wilderness in this complete 14-book mountain man saga!

Holding on to the dream of living in the Rocky Mountains that Tatum shared with his father, he begins his journey—a journey that takes him through the lands of the Osage and Kiowa and ultimately to the land of the Comanche. Now he has a family, and the wilderness makes many demands on anyone that tries to master the mountains…

"Rundell's Rocky Mountain Saint series is marvelous and inspiring." **– Reader**

Follow Tate Saint, man of the mountains, on his journey from boyhood to manhood where he faces everything from the wilds of the wilderness to forces of nature and historic wars.

Rocky Mountain Saint: The Complete Series includes – Journey to Jeopardy, Frontier Freedom, Wilderness Wanderin', Mountain Massacre, Timberline Trail, Pathfinder Peril, Wapiti Widow, Vengeance Valley, Renegade Rampage, Buffalo Brigade, Territory Tyranny, Winter Waifs, Mescalero Madness and Dine' Defiance.

AVAILABLE NOW

ABOUT THE AUTHOR

Born and raised in Colorado into a family of ranchers and cowboys, **B.N. Rundell** is the youngest of seven sons. Juggling bull riding, skiing, and high school, graduation was a launching pad for a hitch in the Army Paratroopers. After the army, he finished his college education in Springfield, MO, and together with his wife and growing family, entered the ministry as a Baptist preacher.

Together, B.N. and Dawn raised four girls that are now married and have made them proud grandparents. With many years as a successful pastor and educator, he retired from the ministry and followed in the footsteps of his entrepreneurial father and started a successful insurance agency, which is now in the hands of his trusted nephew. He has also been a successful audiobook narrator and has recorded many books for several award-winning authors. Now finally realizing his lifelong dream, B.N. has turned his efforts to writing a variety of books, from children's picture books and young adult adventure books, to the historical fiction and western genres which are his first love.

Made in United States
Cleveland, OH
16 February 2025

14399475R10136